Spiders in the Daffodils

NELSON W. PYLES

Burning Bulb

PUBLISHING

Spiders in the Daffodils
By **Nelson W. Pyles**

Burning Bulb Publishing
P.O. Box 4721
Bridgeport, WV 26330-4721
United States of America
www.BurningBulbPublishing.com

Cover designed by Jeanette Andromeda.

First Edition.

Paperback Edition ISBN: 978-0-9977730-9-5

Printed in the United States of America

For Rosemarie Klisiewecz
She believed I could do this before I did.
She always knew and always told me.

PART ONE:
FEAR IN A HANDFUL OF DUST

"Monsters come in all shapes and sizes. Some of them are things people are scared of. Some of them are things that look like things people used to be scared of a long time ago. Sometimes monsters are things people should be scared of, but they aren't." — Neil Gaiman

CHAPTER 1

Romania, 1823

It was just after midnight and Darius Muresan couldn't sleep. He'd gotten into an argument with his wife Sorina and he'd been thinking about it for hours.

This was not typical for Darius.

For one thing, the arguments with Sorina usually were settled calmly, later and in the bedroom with much more pleasant results. In fact, he'd been counting on the usual method of reconciliation this time as well.

Sorina was not having any of it.

He wanted to move out of the country and try his fortunes elsewhere. She simply did not and no matter how Darius worded it, it was not working in his favor.

"What does Slovenia have that we do not have here?" she had asked. It was a very fair question that Darius could not answer. He didn't know, other than he assumed that country wasn't occupied.

"It would be good for the family," he said. "Our sons and daughter will have chances we will never have."

Sorina rolled her eyes and again, this was something that she never did. She was a good, respectful wife, but for some reason she was not cooperating. She'd stormed off after dinner and went to bed. His daughter Viorica took care of the dishes with help from her older brother Theodor. Darius tended to the baby, little Neculas and wondered how angry Sorina was really.

As it turned out, she was furious.

She never yelled when she was truly angry. That would have been too easy and they both knew it. She just glared at him every free chance she had and she was excellent at it. He felt eyes bore into him even from their bed room.

"Poppa, why is mother so angry?" Viorica asked after her mother had stormed off. Darius said nothing and walked outside.

"I know why," Theodor said.

"How do you know?" she asked.

"Because I listen."

She smirked.

"But you do not always hear, brother."

Theodor, who was three years older than his eleven year old sister laughed.

"That is mostly true," he said, stacking the rest of the meager dishes from dinner. "But this time, I did. Father wants us to move."

"Move where? That sounds exciting." She said, getting the dishes ready to wash by the stream.

"I think back to Slovenia, but I am not sure. Out that way I guess."

"Why Slovenia?"

"I have no idea,"

The family had moved from Slovenia to Romania when Viorica was a very little girl. She barely remembered her time there and even less of why they had moved in the first place. Theodor had said that their names at one point were different when they lived there, but had all been changed when they came to Romania. She had asked why, but Theodor claimed ignorance. Viorica knew he was telling the truth because he looked sadly at her when he responded. A lie told by Theodor was told directly in the eye, he had once told her.

Viorica thought about this for a moment and couldn't even think to why they'd go back, but still it was exciting.

They all went to bed early, but Viorica stayed awake for a long time trying to imagine what Slovenia looked like.

She was still awake along with her father, just after midnight.

Darius, was looking again at the ceiling listening to his wife lightly snore and whisper, "I am sorry, my love."

The snoring stopped and she replied, "*This* you whisper?"

He could tell she was smiling.

"And you should not be sorry," she added. "I believe you are right."

Darius rolled over to look at his wife who did the same. It was dark and they couldn't see each other, but they could feel each other. They brought their faces close together to kiss.

"Why did you not say I was right before?" he asked.

"It is my right as your wife to make you think about the decisions you make for us," she said. "And I am afraid of moving, but I believe this time, you are right."

"You are also stubborn." He said and she couldn't argue this point so she kissed him.

"As are you, Darius." She said.

The peace treaty that had begun to take place masked the noises outside of the little house that started shortly thereafter. Viorica has heard it though and woke up Theodor to investigate.

"Let me sleep," he said rolling over. The two siblings shared the bed as Neculas slept quietly in a bassinet near Viorica's side. The bed wasn't that large, but the brother and sister didn't mind.

Except for right now.

"Theodor, you are the closest to the door. It sounds like someone trying to get in the house," she said, getting angry.

"Are you scared?" he asked. "Because you don't have to be scared. I will protect you."

"You can't protect anyone if you are asleep," she said.

Theodor sighed heavily as he heard his parents in the next room.

"I suppose Poppa is not going to look, eh?" he said, sitting up finally.

"That is why I asked you," she said, also sitting up. "I will come with you if you like."

Theodor chuckled.

"No, dear sister. It is my duty to protect the Muresan house." He stumbled as he got out of bed and lurched out of the room.

Viorica did feel a little safer. Her brother was very protective of both of his siblings. She hated to wake him up, but he'd be angry if she had gone to wake up Poppa.

She tried to listen to what her brother was doing, but it was hard because she could hear her mother and father getting louder and louder. She shook her head.

She heard her brother open the door and say something quietly. She heard a hitting sound followed by a very loud thud. She jolted back up in her bed.

She heard footsteps come into the house. Her heart began to pound.

She heard her father in the next room throw open his door.

"Who are you?" she heard him yell. A very calm voice responded in another language. After a moment, she heard her father say something in another language she couldn't recognize.

Next she heard her mother come out of the room. She screamed her brother's name.

Viorica jumped out of bed and ran to the bedroom door, but did not open it. She heard her father speaking in that other language to someone and they were responding. But she heard something in her father's voice she'd never heard before.

Fear.

Darius was a very large strong man; decades of farming had made him one of the biggest men in her village and he sounded afraid.

She opened the door a fraction to see what was happening.

She saw her mother, kneeling over Theodor, who wasn't moving. She was sobbing.

Suddenly, the door was yanked out of her hand. She stood there as a man she'd never seen before looked at her and smiled.

"Ah, the daughter!" the man said in her language. "Come on out. I do not bite."

Before she could protest, the man yanked her into the main room. She saw her father who was wide eyed. She looked at the man and frowned.

"Who are you?" she asked.

"Ask your father," he said.

"Poppa?"

The fear in her father's face was replaced with a look she had also never seen. Shame.

"Poppa?" she said again.

He looked at her and shook his head.

"Don't," Darius said, but not to her.

"Keeping secrets has brought us here, is that not right, Dragan?" the man said.

"Stop it," Darius said. The fear returned to his eyes, but now with a little anger mixed in.

"Poppa, I do not understand."

"Quiet now, Viorica." Darius said. "Let me handle this,"

"Oh, I am so sorry Dragan." The man said, still holding Viorica's arm. "But the time for you to have handled this is long past overdue. I will now handle it."

He looked at the terrified little girl.

"I think I will start here," he said.

"Please! Do not kill her!" Darius cried.

"You have my word, I will not kill her," the man replied. "I will not even kill you."

Darius steeled himself. He knew that he was a man of his word, but there was always a catch.

The man lifted Viorica by her arm as she screamed in pain and fear.

He brought her right up to his face. She looked him in the eyes and he smiled. She watched as his smile seemed to grow.

And grow.

His smile grew until his lips bloodlessly tripped in a line straight up to his ears. The jawline distended and the teeth began to transform into sharpened jagged knives. His face began to change color to a pale, faded black. Viorica was horrified but found herself unable to breathe, much less scream.

Darius on the other hand, had more than enough scream for everyone. Sorina was still on the floor, attending to her son and did not look at her daughter.

"Allow me to introduce you to your future," the snarling man said and bit into her face. Darius lurched forward a foot but then stopped. The little girl was unable to scream, but violently shook as the man began drinking her blood. She began to pass out and the man dropped her. Her last memory was the man squatting over her, biting a wound into his arm and holding it to her lips.

"Drink deeply," he said and she fell into the blackness.

Viorica began to stir, not knowing what had happened. She remembered having a nightmare and being afraid. She opened her eyes slowly and realized she was on the floor near the table.

"Poppa?" she said.

Silence.

She realized her face hurt and put a hand up to it. She didn't feel anything, but it still hurt as if she had been struck.

"I am afraid I lied to you," a voice said in the room. "I do bite, but only when I need to,"

The memory of what had happened flooded back to her at the sound of his voice and Viorica sat up quickly.

"Poppa!" she said.

A hand reached her head and began to stroke it gently.

"Shhhh," the man said. "All in time. First, you must stand up Viorica."

Scared though she was, she listened to the man and carefully stood up. She could tell it was dark; still night time, but she could see everything clearly. This struck her as strange as there were no candles lit in the small shack.

"Yes, it is still night," The man said. "You have new eyes among other things."

She looked around the room until her eyes fell on the man standing next to her.

He was tall with light hair. He was handsome, but his eyes...they were blue and somehow glowing at her. He smiled at her, but it wasn't his smile when he bit her. It was a regular big smile and it was the most terrifying thing she had ever seen.

But, her first reaction wasn't to cower. She snarled at him and this too, terrified her.

"Good!" he said. "You learn fast, *cel mic*. And there are so many more things to learn!"

"I do not understand," she said, recoiling from him. "Where is my family?"

"I am your family now," he said. "I am Stephan but you may call me father."

"Where is my father? Where is my mother?" she said shaking her head.

"You will get to say goodbye, but you must realize that your past is dead."

"I do not want to say goodbye, I want *my* family!"

She pulled away from him and snarled again. She ran for the front door, but suddenly, Stephan was there waiting. She recoiled and ran to the other end of the shack.

Except she arrived there much quicker than she had ever thought possible. Not stopping to question it, she tore the door open and ran. She ran so quickly that when she did stop, her shack was almost impossible to see. She had cleared what seemed like miles in seconds. She could not believe her eyes.

She looked around and saw clearly in the darkness. She saw the Carpathian Mountains clear as day, and could see farther than she thought possible.

She heard sounds she'd never heard before; she smelled things never sensed.

Then, Stephan arrived, snapping her reverie.

"The whole world is a new place, is it not?" he said. "I can barely remember how the world used to look with human eyes."

"What did you do?"

"I have saved you," he said proudly. "You are not a mere girl. You are part of the darkness you have feared your whole life. It is my gift to you,"

She look at him.

"I do not want this," she said.

Stephan frowned.

"Shame," he said. "So, I should kill you now?"

She backed away a few steps.

"I want my family," She said.

Stephan smiled.

"They are all in the house you ran from," he said. "Now when you run back, you are going to be very *very* hungry. You will eat what I have prepared for you."

She looked at him puzzled.

"I'm not hungry," she said.

"You will be when you go back to your home." He said.

"I don't-"

His face changed into the snarling rictus it had been when he had bitten her and she shrieked. She ran towards her home, screaming the whole way. She arrived in seconds, and when she did, she could smell something coppery and hot just outside of the door. It smelled inviting.

"Go in," Stephan's voice said, although he wasn't anywhere near her.

She paused, panting again from the exertion. And worse, she found that she was hungry.

Very hungry.

She opened the door.

No candles were lit, but she could see her family.

They were lying on the floor, twitching. Her mother and father, her brother Theodor and the baby. The baby seemed to be the only one not bleeding and something in her snapped.

It wasn't anger or fear.

It was hunger.

Her whole being began to vibrate as she felt herself change. Transform.

She felt her mouth extend and her jaw unhinge itself. Her teeth grew sharp but that wasn't the worst of it. Her bones felt like they were splitting apart from each other; her skin crumpled away like an old coat and fell to the floor. Her legs grew, her knees sharply bending the other way. Her whole physical self, transformed into...

Something else.

Something hungry.

She looked again at the pile of people that was once her family, who now were trying to crawl away from her. She looked at her baby brother Neculas.

As if in a dream, she saw her arms shoot out toward the baby, but they weren't her arms. They were the long black talon tipped things from a nightmare. They grabbed the baby and held it him up to her face. Without considering it, she ate the baby whole, feeling it wiggle in her mouth until she bit down once, twice and swallowed.

She licked her lips and grabbed her brother Theodor, who weakly tried to fight back. He held his fists up in front of him, but she bit into them and with a jerk of her head, tore them both off just above the wrists. He screamed. She chewed and swallowed his hands. She then bit off the head and most of her brother's upper torso. The blood sprayed out like a geyser.

This repeated with her parents until there was nothing left but sticky hot blood, gristle and torn flesh covering the floor. She ate all of them and did not stop until the only sound was that of a faint dripping sound.

This sound came from her own mouth.

Having been satiated, she looked around the shack at what her life had been.

"You did exceedingly well," Stephan said from the doorway. "Now, you can change back."

Viorica growled.

"You need to calm down and picture yourself as you were. *Concentrate*."

Viorica growled again, but closed her eyes. She tried to focus on how she looked the last time she saw herself in a mirror and eventually, she could. She began to vibrate again as her body slowly at first, began to change and snap into place. It wasn't painful, but it was disconcerting. The last thing to change was a sheen of skin forming over her bones which itched more than anything.

When the vibrations stopped, she opened her eyes.

She could see in the dark even better than she had. She felt strong. Powerful.

She brought her arms up to see and saw that they looked like had before the change. The skin was a bit more pink than usual, but she looked as she always looked.

She realized she was now naked and ran to her room to find clothes. She grabbed a dress and found her boots. She put them on in silence and turned to see her reflection.

She was her old self.

She walked out of the room and saw Stephan waiting for her. He was smiling.

He was standing in a puddle of blood and gore.

Blood and gore that had been...

No.

No.

The gravity of what she had become shifted into the gravity of what she had just done. She began to weep and dropped to her knees.

She had slaughtered her family without hesitation.

She had *devoured* her family without hesitation.

Her cries came in heaving sobs as Stephan moved closer to her, but said nothing for a while.

"You are a new *thing*, Viorica," he said not unkindly. "You must walk away from your past and who you were. From *what* you were and concentrate on what you are now."

"What am I?" she said. "A monster?"

"You are something akin to a *strigoi*," he began. "But there isn't really a word for what we are. We are alive, not dead. We are not human, but look like them to those passing by. We are more like a *paianjen*, a spider in some ways. You are a predator. You are...superior."

"I have killed my family," she said, hearing Stephan and not hearing at the same time.

"You have *survived*," Stephan corrected. "Your family ceased the moment you became what you are. Now, come. We must leave."

Viorica recoiled.

"I will go *nowhere* with you," she said crawling backward away from him. "I will never go anywhere with you!"

Stephan's expression darkened.

"If you want to live, you will come with me," he said. "Do you want to kill your entire village? Any more family around here? You'll eat them all. You don't know how to control yourself and if you don't come with me, I'll let you slaughter everyone here. You will beg me to kill you."

She looked at him. With her new heightened senses, she could tell he was telling the truth. As much as she hated him, this monster, she knew she needed to go with him.

"Gather some things and meet me outside," he said, turning to walk out of the door. "Take a moment to say goodbye to your life as it was."

He closed the door hard.

She sat and cried.

She felt hollow and cold inside.

CHAPTER 2

Tom Wall sat on the river bank with his fishing pole in hand. He looked across to the other bank to see a deer drinking and he smiled. A gentle tap on his shoulder and a pointed finger to the deer followed. Tom looked up at the smiling face standing behind him. It was covered in hair and vaguely looked like him.

"Ain't that beautiful?" the man said, sitting down next to Tom.

"Sure is Pa," Tom said.

Every Sunday that Tom could remember, his Pa would take him fishing along the river that ran not a mile from their little shack in the woods. And for as many times as he went, he always saw something new and beautiful. It was his favorite time with his Pa and from all accounts, it seemed like it was his Pa's favorite time too.

For the past hour, the morning mist had been slowly burning off of the lake's water. There was always something to see after the fog cleared. Sometimes it was like this deer. Sometimes, it was something else.

One time, they saw a Grizzly bear with two baby bears on the opposite side of the river bank. Usually the sight of a Grizzly would have sent them packing, but the way Arthur Wall looked at was "Hell, they's out fishin' just like us. They ain't comin' over here, and we sure ain't going over there,"

Tom agreed wholeheartedly.

But this morning was different. It felt better than it usually did and Tom smiled unrestrained. So did his Pa.

They fished for about another hour, caught about a dozen bass and a few sunfish which was a pretty good haul, and decided to head home. They stopped off at home to clean the fish and leave them with Tom's Ma to get ready for curing and cooking for supper later on in the day.

"Make sure you get some flour, my lovelies." Ma said, the echo of her life in Ireland still lingering on her lips. "And say hi to Stella Arlen if ya see her."

Tom and his Pa walked towards town, holding hands. It was a fine day.

"You left your gun home, Pa." Tom said, noticing that his Pa had his holster, but missing the Colt.

"Ah, it don't matter none," his Pa said. "I ain't never had need to pull it out in town. I doubt anybody's gonna be ornery on a day like this."

That answer seemed to suit Tom just fine.

Tom's Pa was a big man, easily over six feet tall and muscular in build. He made his money from farming and odd labor jobs in and around Murfreesboro. He'd been a soldier in the war and managed to not get killed for his trouble. Since the reconstruction, he'd taken to keeping a sidearm with him, but the last few years, he'd begun to relax. He did his work, kept food on his family's plates and had so very few complaints.

And fewer enemies, especially in Murfreesboro.

When Tom and his Pa strode into town, they were greeted by a collection of smiling faces and waves from the other folks who lived in and around Murfreesboro. They saw Doc Hamley, who was really getting up there in years, but still spry enough to be headed into the Saloon before eleven. He waved and gave a quick, if not genuine smile as he walked into the darkened drinking palace.

The two walked past a few more buildings until they reached Arlen's Livery and Mercantile. There was a horse and cart in front being loaded by Dillon Arlen, the owner and a huge black man known only as Tree. There were several theories as to why he was called tree, the most believable one was that he was so damned tall. He had long, muscular arms and was, "as strong as a goddamn oak" as the tale went. Tree saw Tom and his Pa and smiled.

"Well, y'all strollin' into town after what seems like a couple years " he said in a deep booming voice. Arlen looked up and smiled as well.

"Hell fire, Artie. It's been a few." He said, depositing a load of feed onto the cart. "And you brung the boy I see. How old are you now, Tom?"

"About nine I reckon," Tom said and Tree laughed.

"Listen to him talkin' like he's an adult." Tree said. "He 'reckons' he's nine."

Tom's Pa laughed too, but Tom wasn't too amused. His Pa put a hand on his shoulder and said "They don't mean nothin' son. They just ain't seen you in a while."

Dillon saw the look in Tom's eyes and smiled even broader.

"Your Pa is right, Tom. Hell, you look like you growed a dang foot and then some since last I seen you, ain't that right Tree?"

Tree nodded.

"Yes sir, at least that much. Gonna be one tall hombre, that one there."

This seemed to coax a smile out of Tom.

"Y'all know what you need, you can start grabbin' it inside. Me and Tree are gonna finish up here and be inside in a few. The wife'll be happy to see you boys. Might even have a cookie or somethin' for Tom."

"I *reckon* she just might," Tree said and Dillon laughed. Tom ran into the store and his Pa followed close behind as the two men set back to work.

Inside, Tom's Pa saw Nicole Arlen smiling and hugging Tom tightly.

"Well, just look at ya, boy! Grown like a weed!" she said. Tom hugged her back, but was blushing and uncomfortable. Mrs. Arlen was legendary in Murfreesboro for being quite the eye turner, even at the age of fifty. The locals all said if you didn't have an eye for Mrs. Arlen, you most certainly were blind. Long blonde hair tied in a rope, a floral bonnet and a dress tight enough to see her ribs while breathing.

"Howdy, Mrs. Arlen." Tom's Pa said smiling. She winked at him.

"Why, Arthur Wall. You don't have to be that polite now do ya?" she said. "How's your lovely Missus, Franny?"

"She's good. Said to say howdy as well."

"Well, I seriously doubt that a fine woman like yours would ever use howdy in conversation but tell her a hearty howdy back."

"I sure will." He said. "I came to pick up a few items if that's alright,"

She smiled a grand smile.

"Ah, not a social call, eh?" She laughed. "Come over here and tell me what you need."

They walked over to the counter, Tom in tow.

"Tom, go in the back there and fetch yourself a cookie. One for you and one for your old man if you wouldn't mind," Mrs. Arlen said.

There was no need to tell him twice; he bolted for the back room quickly.

"That's boy is fast! Spitting image of your missus, Art."

"Yeah, he's a good boy." He said proudly. "It's a damn treat watchin' him grow up. Goes so damn fast, though."

"Well, you don't need me to tell you, but you do right by that boy. He's gonna be one hell of a man one day." She leaned in. "My Maria is around the same age…she'd make a fine wife one day."

"Sounds like you may need to talk to the missus sooner than later." He said, smiling.

She laughed.

"We'll be here, Art Wall. They won't be getting married any time soon," She said and picked up a pen.

***

Tom found the cookies almost immediately. They were huge, sugar cookies which were Tom's favorite (*although any cookie at all from Mrs. Arlen was his favorite cookie. His Ma's cookies were nowhere near as good, or big.*) He couldn't count, but he knew one for him and one for his Pa so he grabbed two on the top.

He debated eating his right then and there when he heard a gunshot, followed by yelling and two more gunshots. He ducked down, dropping the cookies. He heard his Pa yell something and then he heard another two gunshots. Tom's mouth dropped open and he began to shake. He didn't hear anything for a few moments and then he heard a sound like someone chopping a melon. Direct, stead mushy sounding hits. He heard a dark, deep harsh laugh. Tom steadied himself and stood up. Carefully, he walked to the opening that lead out to the mercantile floor. He peeked out of the curtain and gasped.

Mrs. Arlen was slumped over the counter, bleeding from her head. It looked like part of the top of her head was missing and Tom had to fight to keep what little he had in his stomach. The hitting noise was coming from the other side of the counter. He could see a hand raise up with something in it and quickly drop down, connecting to something…wet.

It had to be his Pa, taking care of whoever did this to Mrs. Arlen. He slowly crept out of the back room and looked carefully around the counter.

15

It was his Pa.

But not doing the hitting.

There was a big man on his knees, hitting his Pa in the face repeatedly with the side of a pistol. However, anything that resembled his father's face seemed to have somehow slid off of his skull which was beginning to collapse from the repeated hits. Tom's mouth opened wide and he let out a scream that came from the very center of him. The big man who had killed his father looked at the boy and smiled. He didn't bother to stop hitting his Pa.

"Don't worry ya damn pup," he said. "You're *next*."

Tom, still screaming, ran back into the room behind the mercantile and out of the back door. He began to regret it immediately as soon as the sunlight hit his face. He should do something. He should grab something and hit that man, like he hit his Pa.

He stopped. He squeezed his eyes closed to figure something out.

Tom had heard five gunshots. The gun (*now beating his Pa*) looked like a Patterson Colt; same gun his Pa had with its long barrel. If it was that, it only had five bullets in it, so that wasn't a problem.

He turned and started back to the mercantile. He looked for something, like a stick or a shovel. From where he was however, he could see the front of the mercantile. He saw the dead bodies of Mr. Arlen and Tree. Both were dead and bleeding in the street. He tried to stay steady, but he was failing. He'd never been more terrified than he was right now.

His Pa...

As he stepped into the back room again, he saw a pitchfork leaning against the wall next to the door. He grabbed it. He heard the man, still hitting, breathing heavy and swearing.

Pa...

Tom held the pitchfork and walked straight through the door and right up to the man. His arm was raised to his poor Pa again. Tom looked at the gun, suspended in the air and he saw with certainty that it was, a Patterson Colt.

The killer was about to say something when Tom Wall charged and jammed the pitchfork right into the man's face.

"Goot," the man said. At least, that's what it sounded like to Tom. Two of the metal spikes entered both of eyes and Tom pushed hard. They went on about three inches when he heard the man say, "*Goot.*"

The man slowly began to fall forward and pushed Tom back from the free falling dead weight. He struggled to keep him up; he didn't want that man to fall on his Pa, but it was a losing battle. Tom let the fork go, and to his surprise, kept the man from falling down all the way. Tom stood there a moment, looking at what he'd done. He nodded, as if agreeing he'd done the right thing.

Then, he looked down at his Pa and began to cry. He dropped to his knees next to his Pa, and looked at him. He tried to look at where his face was, but it was too hard and he tried to imagine what he looked like. His face wouldn't come into his head and he wept bitterly. He screamed again and buried his face into his Pa's chest.

He lay like that for a very long time.

***

Three Years Later

Tom was still on the floor in the barn where he slept. It was still pitch black outside and damn, it was cold. Tennessee was awful cold in February and the snow still falling outside didn't much help. He had two burlap sacks covering him and the hay beneath him helped keep him warmer, but not much. He wouldn't freeze to death he knew, but it still felt like dying.

He chose to sleep in the barn about seven months earlier, when it was decidedly much warmer. He didn't regret his decision; the man his Ma took up with last year hadn't run off like he'd hoped he would and it was just too awful for Tom to stay in that house too long while he was around.

She met Pepper Jackson last year and he was plenty nice at first, but he got real bad. He had a mean streak that appeared one day and hadn't left since. Tom couldn't reckon what had turned him sour at first, until his Ma broke down one day and told him.

It was her talking about his Pa. Even worse was that she told Pepper about what Tom did *after* his Pa died. Pepper became nervous being around Tom. Not nervous enough, since that's also around the time he started beating Tom. He'd talk to him, while hitting him, daring him to try something.

"You best not think you can just kill a man like that," Pepper said, hitting Tom in the back with a knotted plough line. "You best *know* you can't come at *me* like that!"

It was brutal and excruciating for Tom, but after a while, he learned to shut it out. The last time Pepper tried to lay into him, Tom just took it. He refused to cry. Bit his lip if he needed to, and took it. When Pepper was done, Tom stood up and just looked at Pepper dead in the eye.

Pepper didn't hit him again.

Tom hit his threshold when Pepper hit his Ma one day, out of nowhere in the kitchen. She was frying up a squirrel for supper when he came in, drunk and hungry.

"Where's my supper?" he said.

"It'll be a few minutes," she said. "Just finishing up the squirrel. Have a seat."

He grabbed her shoulder and punched her in the face, knocking her and the pan with the squirrel to the hard floor.

Tom, who was sitting at the table, stood up angry. Pepper whirled at him.

"Don't you goddamn think about it, boy." He said. "You sit down or I'll give her another wallop."

Tom glared at him and he saw that whatever Pepper saw in his eyes, shook him a little. He backed up a little, but repeated it.

"I'll hit her, if you keep goin', goddamn it. *Sit!*"

Reluctantly, Tom sat, but the look never left his face.

Later that night, Tom told his Ma he was going to sleep in the barn.

"I don't know why, Tom." She said crying. "This is your home."

"It ain't while he's here Ma," he said. "He's gonna hit you to get at me and that ain't right. But I'll be able to hear what's going on just in case."

"Just in case of what?" she asked, but Tom didn't reply. He just kissed his Ma, and walked out to the barn.

That was July. Now, it was February and he shivered so hard, he couldn't fall back asleep. He tried to think about his Pa and what he'd do if he were him.

Pa never would have let this happen, he thought. *He'd have throwd Pepper out straight away.* He nodded to himself.

He then thought of all the times he'd gone fishing with his Pa. All the little talks they'd have about everything and nothing. They were, as near as tom could recall, the best things in his life.

Gone in minutes.

He fought back a tear. Crying wasn't practical anymore. Crying slowed you down. You couldn't think if you were crying, so crying had to go. There wasn't a way back, just forward. And there wasn't a forward with Pepper around. That was for damn sure.

Tom had grown physically in the last three years. He was twelve, but he looked much older. He was tall at almost six feet and he had a strong wiry muscular frame. He was twelve, but he looked like a man. The glare he had given to Pepper that one day was now his fixed expression. Tom wasn't mean, or cruel, but that look damn near told people different. He would only lose the expression if it were just him and his Ma, which wasn't too often.

He shivered again and this time he decided he'd go into the house to warm up a little bit. Maybe see if there was a biscuit or something as well. He got up and stretched. He opened the barn door and looked at the horizon. The sun was on its way, but it was still at least another hour away from rising. He walked slowly towards the house and quietly opened the door to the kitchen.

It was a very small house; only three rooms. The heat from the wood burning was welcome and he closed the door to hunker in front of it. He rubbed his hands together and let the warmth envelop him. It was a full minute before he stood back up and looked around for something to eat.

He hadn't noticed when he first walked in, but his eyes adjusted and he saw the kitchen was nearly in pieces. One of the chairs was broken nearly in half and lying on the floor. How had he not heard that? He walked through the room and took a look around. He nearly tripped on something and he stopped. He looked down and saw something dark on the floor. He bent down.

It was Ma.

She wasn't moving, or breathing. It was too dark to see her face, but he saw her eyes were open; the fire from the stove reflected in them. He looked at them for a long time before he took his hand and closed them.

He knew two things. His Ma was dead and Pepper had killed her. He still couldn't believe he didn't hear anything. He'd worry about that later. For now, he also knew Pepper wasn't in the house. It was puzzling. He pushed aside the desire to cry, and tried to think.

Pepper wasn't a quiet or shy man. His anger was quick and loud. How could he kill his Ma quietly when he hadn't done anything quiet in his whole life?

When Tom went to bed, Pepper and Ma weren't even home. They'd gone into town for a drink, which come to think of it, almost never happened. In fact, it had never happened. Not even once.

So, when did they get home, and when did Pepper leave?

And when was he coming back, assuming he would come back?

What if he killed her while they were out, brought her back here and left? Why would he do that?

He started mulling these things around all while fighting the urge to break down. He was angry and sad, but determined to figure this out, because now it was all he had. He decided he'd have to leave the house and head into town. That meant leaving Ma on the floor of the house, which he didn't want to do.

He found the matches on the counter and lit up the only oil lantern they had; the bright light cut through the blackness and he'd be able to see her clearly. He took a deep breath and looked down at her.

He could see her neck had been cut straight across, but there wasn't a lot of blood. She'd been killed outside of the house and brought back inside.

Tom didn't really know how he knew this, but it made the most sense. He was *thinking* and not crying. He was steady and he put the lantern down. He bent down and picked his mother up. She'd been very thin the last few months, and she was lighter than he thought she'd be. He gently took her into the bedroom and put her on top of the covers. He felt around for a blanket at the bottom of the bed and covered her body. He moved close to her head and gently kissed it.

"I love you, Ma." He said quietly. He fought crying one last time and stood up.

He covered her face with the blanket and turned to go back to the kitchen. He stood there not quite knowing what he was going to do next, but he knew one thing he'd need.

***

Valerian Cobb stood in front of the Murfreesboro sheriff's office and jail on a bright, crisp March morning. The coach he'd arrived on was headed to the local livery so the horses could rest and the driver could as well. He wasn't going to be there long, but long enough to see what he'd come to see. It hadn't snowed in weeks, but the town was still in its blanket. It looked pretty enough. Cobb liked to notice such things, but kept them to himself if only so the moment, however small, could be his and his alone.

He spit and walked up to the door, knocking before walking inside.

The sheriff was a portly man about fifty, half sitting, half falling out of his chair. There was a wood stove so hot, it was almost glowing. In the cell that took up a fourth of the office, was Tom Wall, fast asleep as well.

Cobb closed the door hard and it startled both the sheriff and Tom.

"Jesus H Christ," the sheriff said, nearly falling out of his chair. "Gonna give me a goddamn heart attack."

"You Sheriff Tate?" Cobb said flatly.

"Who the hell are you?"

"I'm Captain Cobb, Texas Rangers." Cobb said. "I got your telegraph and came at your request."

"Well, I'll be," Tate said. "You got here quicker than I thought."

"Is that the boy?"

"That's the killer,"

Cobb nodded.

"I want to talk to him."

"Well, go on ahead." Tate said, settling back into his chair.

"Alone."

"I'm afraid I can't do that," Tate said, standing up.

"I'm afraid you're going to have to get the hell out of your sleepin' chair Sheriff." Cobb said, never taking his eyes off of Tom.

"You can't just barge in here and make demands like that, Ranger."

Cobb looked at Tate and smiled.

"Your telegraph said it was Texas Ranger business," Cobb said. "Well, the Texas Ranger is here to conduct that business and to see if you haven't just wasted my goddamn time. So, if you don't mind, get on out, Sheriff."

Tate was about to say something, but he saw that Cobb meant it in a way that needed no further explanation. He grabbed his heavy jacket, put it on and left the office without saying a word.

Cobb took one of the chairs leaning next to the office door and dragged it over to the cell. He sat down and looked at Tom. He said nothing, just looking at the boy.

Tom sat on the bunk and looked back, scowling.

"They treatin' you right in here?" Cobb asked.

"I reckon," Tom said.

"How old are you?"

"Twelve. Going to be thirteen in March."

"March what?"

"Fifteen."

"Well, I hate to tell you this, but happy birthday."

Cobb smiled.

Tom did not.

"It's March?"

"It is. How long you been in here?"

Tom swallowed.

"Since second week of February,"

"Ain't nobody come for you?"

"No, sir. Ain't nobody *to* come for me."

Cobb nodded.

"I reckon that makes sense. No other kin?"

Tom shook his head.

"You're Art Wall's son."

Tom nodded.

"Did you know him?" Tom asked.

"I did a long time ago," Cobb said. "We was in the war together. He was one of my men."

"Really?"

"He was a good man. I heard what happened to him. Goddamn shame."

Tom didn't know what to say.

"You saw the whole thing, didn't you?"

Tom nodded.

"What were you, eight? Nine?"

"Nine."

Cobb shook his head.

"Damn, son. That's hard." Cobb said. "And you killed that son of a bitch. With a pitchfork, is that right?"

Tom nodded.

"Why didn't you run?"

"He killed my Pa,"

Cobb shook his head.

"Revenge?"

Tom hesitated.

"I never really thought about it. I seen this man killed four people with a five round Patterson Colt. It was empty and he was still hittin' Pa even though he was already dead."

"How'd you know it was a five round gun?"

"Pa had the same gun," Tom said. "I can count up to ten, and I reckoned he was out."

Cobb nodded.

"Did you know who that man was?"

"No sir," Tom said. "Didn't much care to."

"His name was Pete Willey. He was wanted in three states including Texas for horse theft and murder. There was a reward. You know that?"

Tom shook his head.

"Pepper Jackson. Tell me about him."

"What about him?" Tom said. "He's dead."

"He sure as hell is," Cobb said. "That's why I'm here. Jackson was wanted too. Been looking for him for about two years, so imagine when I get word that he'd been killed. By a kid no less. A kid your sheriff wants remanded to the Republic of Texas."

"Why?"

"Your sheriff I reckon, doesn't seem to think the state of Tennessee will put a twelve year old kid on trial for murder and then hang him." Cobb said. "If you ask me, he's just being goddamn lazy."

Tom put his head down.

"So, you're gonna take me to Texas?"

"We'll see." Cobb said. "But I need you to explain a few things."

"He killed my Ma,"

"I know," Cobb said softly. "You look an awful lot like her."

"You knew her too?"

"I did."

Tom lifted his head.

"He cut her neck. Not in the house, but somewhere else, then brought her home. He tried makin' it look like I done it."

Cobb nodded.

"I put her in bed, and got my Pa's gun from the kitchen. I followed Pepper's tracks for a mile or so until I found him."

"How'd you know he did all that? He tell you?"

Tom shook his head.

"Figured it out. When I found him, he had blood all over him that weren't his. He had this big knife he always had strapped to his leg. It was bloody too."?

"How'd you see all this in the dark? The tracks and the blood? It was right before sun up, way I heard it."

"My eyes is okay seein' in the dark," Tom said. "Besides, he had a pretty big fire goin'."

"What did he do when he saw you?"

"Nothin'," Tom said and looked Cobb in the eye. "I shot him in the face."

Cobb nodded. He looked on the boy's face and saw a set of cruel eyes and stern resolve. It wasn't revenge on his face. It was the look of a man who did what he believed was the right thing.

And as far as Cobb could tell, Tom Wall wasn't wrong.

"You went ahead and killed that man based on what you thought had happened," Cobb said.

"He killed my Ma," Tom said. "Weren't much thought needed, figurin' on all I found out."

"Why not go to the sheriff?"

"You met the sheriff. Would *you* go to him?"

Cobb didn't try to hide his smile.

"You're damn near a detective, son. Know that?"

Tom shrugged his shoulders.

"I'm an orphan. And a killer."

Cobb nodded. He reached into his shirt pocket and pulled out a half smoked cigarillo. He took a match from his vest pocket and struck it off of one of the cell bars. He inhaled deeply and blew out the smoke.

"That all you want to be?"

Tom looked at him blankly.

"I was asked to come here to review your problems, Tom. The sheriff thinks I ought to take you to Texas. Put you on trial for this latest killing." He smiled. "Like I said, Tennessee don't want to get their hands dirty I reckon."

"I ain't never been to Texas," Tom said "And he killed my Ma. Don't that count for nothin'?"

"From what you told me, it counts for plenty." Cobb said. "No other kin?"

"No sir."

Cobb took another drag.

"Can you read?"

"No sir."

"Can't write either then. You can count to ten?"

"Yes sir."

The door to the office opened up, bringing with it a cold shock of air and the sheriff. Tate slammed the door behind him.

"I think I've been patient enough, Cobb." Tate said. "You taking him with you for trial or what?"

Cobb stood up.

"Ain't gonna be no trial, Sheriff."

"He's a killer."

"He's a *boy*."

"He slit his Momma's neck and killed that Pepper Jackson in cold blood," Tate said.

"Not according to him. You actually *talk* to this boy?"

"He's a boy, like you said. Who'd believe anything he'd have to say?"

"I do," Cobb said. "Ain't that why you sent for me? For my assessment?"

"Well," Tate started, but Cobb continued.

"I'm taking this boy into my custody." Cobb said. "Open that goddamn cage up."

Tate looked at him.

"You taking him for trial?"

"I said open the cage," Cobb said. "I'm taking him into custody. First, I'm gonna give this boy a decent meal. Then, I'm taking him with me."

"To trial?" Tate repeated.

"No, to Texas," Cobb replied.

"Now, just a goddamn minute Cobb," Tate said, putting his hand on his gun. Cobb pulled his gun so quickly it took Tate a moment to realize that he was staring down the barrel. Cobb pulled the hammer back.

"I've had just about enough of your shit," Cobb said through his teeth. "You see that wanted poster behind your desk? How long's it been there?"

Tate put both of his hands up and shrugged his shoulders.

"I don't recall…maybe a year or two?"

"Well, maybe if you had been payin' attention, you'd have recognized Pepper fucking Jackson maybe a year or two ago and saved this boy from his troubles."

Tate's eyes darted towards his desk, but Cobb stopped him.

"No, you look here. I ain't done talking to you," he snarled. "Now, you open that goddamn cell and let that boy the hell out of there or I'll make sure he sues the hell out of you for wrongful imprisonment."

Tate snickered.

"Where the hell is he gonna get that kind of money?" Tate said. "He ain't got a pot to piss in as it is."

"That's where you're wrong," Cobb said. "Seeing as he singlehandedly took care of the man who killed his Daddy, a wanted fugitive and *this* son of a bitch, *also* a wanted man, he's due reward money of about two thousand dollars. I'm going to take him to collect that money. I'd rather he start saving money now than suing your sorry ass, but I reckon that'll really be up to him. Personally, I'd like to see that boy whip your ass like there's no tomorrow. But instead, you're gonna open that goddamn cage or *I'm* gonna whip your ass."

"You can't do that," Tate said. "This ain't Texas. You're outta your jurisdiction."

Cobb lowered the hammer on his gun and put it in the holster. Then, he grabbed Tate by the collar and nearly pulled him off of his feet."

"I *am* Texas," he said sternly. "And my jurisdiction is anywhere I happen to be."

Tate, knowing he'd pushed his luck at last, scrambled his belt ring until he found the keys. He held them up to Cobb so he'd see them, and he let Tate go. Tate staggered over to the cell and clumsily unlocked the cell door. He pulled it open.

Tom stood there, stunned at what he'd just seen in front of him. He looked at Cobb, who nodded.

"You hungry, boy?" he said.

Tom nodded.

Tate had backed away from the two as Tom slowly came out of the cell.

"You're a big 'un, ain't ya?" Cobb said.

"Yes sir," Tom said.

"Well," Cobb said. "Let's go get you a breakfast or two."

Cobb looked at the sheriff.

"Where's this boy's coat?"

"He ain't got one." Tate said.

Cobb looked and saw a couple of coats on a hook. He reached into his pocket and pulled out ten dollars. He threw it on the floor and grabbed the biggest coat he could find on the hook. He handed it to Tom who put it on.

"Now, where's the gun you took off of this boy?"

Tate hurried over to the desk and pulled open a drawer. He pulled the gun out and carefully brought it to Cobb, holding it out.

Cobb reached out and yanked it out of Tate's hand.

He glared at Tate.

"Do yourself a favor and retire. Soon." He said, and led Tom outside.

***

Cobb and Tom walked up the street slowly. The coat was just a little big on Tom, but it was warm. His head was pointed down as they walked.

"Well kid, where can we get some food? All that bullshit's got me a might hungry."

Tom looked up to see where they were walking and nodded.

"Up the street a piece is the saloon, sir. They got food. I don't know about breakfast."

"Hell, a drink wouldn't hurt either," Cobb said. "But I gotta get some food into you, boy. Long trip ahead."

"Sir," Tom said. "Was that true? About the reward?"

"Damn right," Cobb said. "I was hoping to tell you over some grub, but that ignorant bastard pissed me off."

Tom seemed to regard this for a moment.

"I reckon I can pay you back for breakfast, sir."

Cobb laughed. Ha put an arm around Tom and they stopped.

"Listen son," he said. "Food's on me, the travel is on me too. And you ain't touching that money until you're old enough. I'll keep it safe for you. As of right now, you are in my custody."

Tom went pie eyed.

"I'm your prisoner?" he asked. Again, Cobb laughed.

"No, you ain't no prisoner. Look, you ain't got no kin in this world no more. Me either. But, your Pa was a good man, and your Ma was a hell of a woman. They were done wrong, but not as wrong as was done on *you*. If it's all the same, I'd like to keep an eye on you while you're growin' up. Make sure nothing like what you already been through happens again."

Tom looked at Cobb. His scowl softened, just a little bit.

"I reckon that'd be fine by me, sir." Tom said.

Cobb smiled.

"You are really, *goddamn* polite." Cobb said. He clapped Tom on the shoulder. "C'mon kid. It's colder than well digger's pecker out here."

"*Sir?*" Tom asked. He had no idea what Cobb meant.

"Oh,...I'll tell you when you're older." Cobb said laughing. "Gonna be tough to remember you're only twelve."

"Thirteen, sir." Tom corrected. Cobb laughed again.

They walked up the steps to the saloon and inside, they sat down.

Turns out, they served a hell of a breakfast and Tom practically inhaled a plate of eggs and biscuits with gravy while Cobb ate about the same, just less. Cobb sat and watched the boy eat and smiled.

"I'd say you skip the manners on your end when it comes to food I reckon,"

Tom stopped, with a mouthful of food and put his fork down.

"Sorry, sir." He said, mouth still stuffed.

"Oh hell, I'm just kiddin' you boy. Go on and eat." Cobb said chuckling. "By God, you've earned the right to eat hearty."

Tom slowly resumed eating, but he seemed to be more mindful how he was eating. When he'd finished, he grabbed the glass of milk and downed about half of it. He let out a loud belch that made one of the whores upstairs laugh.

"You want to take a break, or are you good for now?" Cobb said smiling.

"I'm good, sir. Thank you."

"You just rest up a bit. Don't need you pukin' that breakfast back up."

Tom nodded.

"Sir? Was it true what you said back there? About juris...something."

"Jurisdiction?"

"Yes sir. Is it, wherever you are when you're a Texas Ranger?"

Cobb chuckled.

"I got to admit, Tom. That was a little bit of bullshit. Buddy of mine, another ranger, likes to say that whenever he's trackin' someone out of Texas. If you have the stones, you can pull it off. If not...well, you wind up shot or in the local poke. You have to be able to deliver that line in such a way that there ain't a lick of doubt that it ain't true." He laughed. "Cause it sure as *shit* ain't true."

Tom just looked at him.

"Stones?"

"Yeah, stones. Balls, guts...courage in other words."

"Oh, okay."

"Don't worry, boy." Cobb said. "You already got a big pair on you."

"Is it cold in Texas, sir?"

"Christ in burlap sack, *no*. Quicker we get out of here, the warmer we'll be."

"Sir?"

"You gotta quit with the sir all the time,"

"Sorry, sir." Tom said. "Can I be a Texas Ranger?"

Cobb leaned in close and looked Tom in the eye.

"Son, I think you pretty much already *are* one."

***

Seven Years Later

Cobb spit and pulled his gun. He fired one shot. The bottle he was aiming for exploded in Corporal Brady's hand. Brady, never having done something like this, had his eyes shut tightly and looked at his hand when the bottle disintegrated. He was genuinely surprised and relieved that he still had a hand.

Cobb, Brady and Tom were about a mile or so outside of Austin in the wide open, so Cobb's unusual target practice didn't accidentally shoot someone who wasn't there to get shot. It hadn't happened, but of course, Cobb didn't want it to start happening. He always liked to take a couple of Rangers with him to inspire their technique in accuracy.

And of course, to show off.

Tom had always come with Cobb and was quite a fine shot himself, but never liked showing it off. Cobb, on the other hand, did. Which was fine by Tom. In the past seven years, He'd come to look up to Cobb not just for saving his life, but for teaching him things like how to read and write.

And how to be a Texas Ranger.

The Ranger part had come easy for Tom, but the reading and writing was much harder. Still, he learned and had grown into a smart young man. Even less surprising to Cobb, was that he was quickly becoming one of the best Ranger's he'd even seen.

At the age of twenty, Tom had become one of the youngest Rangers, and no one who had seen him in action doubted the reason why. He was efficient, smart and deadly in a fight; gun or no gun.

He was twenty years old.

"You alright, Corporal?" Cobb yelled.

Brady waved his hand that he was okay.

Cobb chuckled.

"I bet that kid just about pissed himself," he said.

Tom let out a quick laugh.

"Yeah, I reckon he might have," Tom said. "Hell, I don't know many who wouldn't."

Cobb looked at him.

"Well, you never did." Cobb said. "You just give that look you got, like you're gonna split somebody's head wide open."

"You gotta admit, sir. It works."

Cobb laughed.

"You better be careful, or somebody might think you got a sense of humor."

Tom allowed a rare smile.

"Don't worry though," Cobb continued. "You're secret's safe with me."

Cobb holstered the gun and looked at Brady, who was still waving.

"Boy, put your damn hand down and get over here," he yelled. Brady dropped his hand and started to run toward Cobb and Tom. Cobb was chuckling still. "I hope I didn't mess up that kid by shooting the bottle."

"Ah, Brady's good. Half the stuff he does is crazy as a shit house rat, and he's still here. A little trick shooting ain't gonna do nothing'."

Brady was panting a little, but seemingly intact as he got closer.

"That was a hell of a shot, Captain." Brady said. He was a little on the heavy side, but far from being fat. He was about ten years older than Tom but somehow looked younger. He had a thin beard but no mustache. The beard did nothing to help his boyish face.

"Thanks, Brady." Cobb said. "You alright? Me and Tom here was wondering if you'd lost some piss between there and here."

Brady laughed.

"Oh, I'm fine Captain." He said. "I was worried for about one second after the gun went off, but I'm okay."

Cobb pointed at his crotch. Brady's smile faded and he looked. Then he laughed.

"I got ya kid," Cobb said.

The two men laughed, but Tom looked away. His expression changed.

"Captain," Tom said quietly.

Cobb looked at Tom and then where Tom was looking.

"What is it?"

"Looks like about three riders, comin' in fast. One of 'em is shot up pretty bad." Tom said.

Brady pulled out a small telescope and aimed it where the two men were looking.

"He's right, Captain." Brady said. Tom was nearly famous for just how good his eyesight was and it was always being questioned and proven whenever it came up. Brady had been around for a lot of them, and it was always impressive every time.

"Course he's right," Cobb said. "Let's ride out and meet 'em. If that one feller is shot up that bad, better to not wait til they're here. Tom, you wanna see if you can grab the Doc?"

"Yes sir," Tom said and ran to his horse. They were only about a half mile from the main Rangers camp in Austin.

"Come on, Corporal." Cobb said getting on his horse and Brady doing the same.

"Be careful sir," Tom yelled as he mounted his horse.

"Hell, that ain't no damn fun!" Cobb yelled back and took off with Brady.

Tom shook his head as he raced toward the camp.

Fun.

Tom didn't get it. This job wasn't supposed to be fun, but Cobb always managed to have fun somehow in most situations. Usually at Tom's expense, which he also didn't get. Cobb was like a Pa to him, and he loved him like one, but Tom didn't know from fun. He liked the work and buried himself in it. He figured he was good at it because he took it damn serious.

But Cobb was good at it too, and had fun. It boggled Tom sometimes when he thought about it.

Fun got you killed out here.

Fun didn't serve purpose to anything.

Fun made you act like a damn fool.

He squinted his eyes and rode faster.

***

Tom rode into the encampment and went straight to the infirmary. He jumped off his horse and went inside. Judging from the sun, it was about nine in the morning.

"Doc Hanson? You up sir?"

Hanson, who was usually up before the rest of the camp hollered that he was in the back of the infirmary. Tom walked through past a few empty beds to the back door. Outside, Hanson was boiling linens and smoking a cigarillo.

"Mornin', Lieutenant." Hanson said.

"Doc, we need you. Some men are riding in here, one of 'em shot up pretty good. Captain said to come get you to meet them on the way in case it's as serious as it looks."

Doc threw his smoke into the fire.

"Well, I reckon I ought to be grateful for this since I goddamn loathe laundering linens." He said. "Let me get my bag and we'll head out. How far out?"

The two men walked hurriedly into the infirmary.

"I reckon they're about two miles from here about now. We should be able to meet up with them right quick if we hurry. I reckon the Captain and Brady ought to have stopped them by now."

Hanson had his bag and side arm ready and nodded.

"Let's go then." He said.

The two men rushed outside, got on horseback and rode off, Tom leading the way.

***

"Something ain't right," Tom said.

Hanson looked and saw very little. Just the way ahead.

"What do you see?"

"Horses," Tom said. "Dead ones."

"How do you know they're dead?"

"'Cause horses don't usually lie down in the middle of the day," Tom said, digging his spurs into his own horse and vaulting ahead. Hanson followed suit to close the gap to what Tom was seeing.

When they arrived, they saw three dead horses, and three bodies among them.

The one body was of Sean Mallory. He was a new recruit in the Rangers, shot to hell. He was the man Tom had seen originally and he was quite dead now; blood still pouring out of his forehead. The other two were Rangers as well; Johnny Farrow and Bill Jones, both seasoned Rangers. Bill's neck was cut open and quite dead, but Johnny was holding on, just barely. He'd been shot a couple times in the chest. Not superficial wounds, but it wouldn't kill him straight away either.

There was no sign of Cobb or Brady, but Tom reckoned that's why Johnny had been left alive.

Tom and Hanson jumped off of their horses and ran to Johnny. Doc pulled out some cloth and put direct pressure on his chest wounds. Tom knelt down to Johnny, who was coughing up blood.

"What happened Johnny?" Tom said "Where's the Captain and Brady?"

"Kiowa," Johnny said through bloody teeth. "We ran past a small group. Had guns, shot up Sean. Followed us while we ran…caught us when we ran into the Captain. They both got took. Shot the rest of us up. Said they'd be waiting to kill more Rangers if we went after 'em…"

"Kiowa?" Tom said. "We done took care of them,"

"Kickin' Fox is with them," Johnny said. "He's out for revenge, Tom."

"I reckon so," Tom said.

The Kiowa tribe had long been a thorn in the side of Texas in general, but it had calmed down the last few years. Tom had come on

33

board toward the end and it was even ugly as it was getting better. He'd seen what they would do to those they captured and he thought carefully about how to handle going after Cobb and Brady.

"He ain't doin' too good, Lieutenant." Hanson said. "We have to move him now if he's got a shot and the move will likely kill him."

Tom nodded.

"Johnny, I know you heard what the Doc said," Tom said. "What can we do for you?"

Johnny coughed.

"If you're gonna go after them, you best get more Rangers," Johnny said. "Which I know you ain't gonna do. They ain't expecting you. Use that."

"What do you want the doc to do for you?"

"He can try to keep me alive long enough til you get back, but that ain't likely. Go, Tom."

Johnny began to cough and Tom looked at Hanson.

"I'll make him comfortable." Hanson said. "If you're gonna go, then go."

Tom nodded and looked at Johnny before standing up.

He went to his horse and checked his side bag.

He had his rifle and a box of ammunition, ammo for his side arm and a knife.

He checked his side arm; his father's Patterson Colt. It was clean and loaded. He jumped on the horse and took off in the direction of where Cobb and Brady had been taken, figuring he'd know what to do once he found them.

***

Cobb counted their captors, about twelve all together. Of course, he couldn't see behind him but he figured they were all in front of him now, maybe a scout or two keeping an eye out for anyone dumb enough to follow them.

Cobb and Brady were tied to two wagon wheels that were lashed to a couple of trees about three miles from where they had been taken. They'd beaten on Brady pretty good and he was still knocked out cold. They were still dressed, which was a good sign for the moment; it meant they weren't going to be skinned. At least, not yet.

Cobb recognized their captor as Kicking Fox, the son of the last chief from the area before the Kiowa had been driven out after the Red River War. Kicking Fox had been spotted in the area, but not much attention was given to him.

Cobb knew this was a mistake from the get go, but he wasn't exactly in charge. His idea had been to go after him and kill him, but that request was denied. He knew that bad decision would bite them in the ass one day, and now here it was, nibbling on his ass in particular.

He looked at Kicking Fox and frowned at him.

"You wanna tell me what you're waitin' for, Kickin' Wolf?" Cobb said.

Kicking Fox looked and glared at him. He walked slowly over to Cobb.

"Are you in such a hurry to scream, Ranger?" he asked in perfect English.

"No, I ain't," Cobb said. "But I ain't fond of waitin' around much either."

Kicking Fox smiled.

"You are the one called Cobb. That one we call Slow Pup." He said, pointing to Brady who was now snoring.

"That right," Cobb said. "What do you call me?"

"It doesn't matter what we call you. We will call you *dead* soon enough."

"Oh, come on. I'd like to think all of y'all came up with a name for me."

"We call you Spitting Snake," Kicking Fox said. "You are quite deadly with your gun. Without, not so much."

"Spittin' Snake, huh?" Cobb laughed. "I kinda like that. It's a damn sight better than Slow Pup."

"Both names well earned," Kicking Fox said. "We now wait for your White Eagle to bring us more Rangers to kill."

Cobb nodded. White Eagle had to be Tom.

"I'm afraid he won't bring you more Rangers to kill today," Cobb said. "If he comes at all, he'll be alone."

"That would be unfortunate," Kicking Fox said.

"For you, goddamn right." Cobb said. "If he comes alone, ain't nobody around to tell him to stop."

"He would be foolish to come alone."

"I ain't saying that ain't true, but you're all in a whole world of shit you ain't ready for."

Kicking Fox laughed.

"We will see."

He turned and said something in Kiowa. Two men came over to Brady and stared stripping Brady's clothes from him. He continued to snore. Cobb struggled against his bonds because he knew what was coming next. He hoped Tom would get there before they did too much damage to Brady.

***

Tom followed the tracks until he saw the first scout. He stopped riding and found a nearby grove that would be difficult to see. It was likely that the scout had seen him, but the scout remained where he was as far as Tom could see. He watched him closely as he reached into his side bag for his rifle.

In a separate pouch, there was an odd looking scope that he quickly attached to the rifle. He looked at the leaves, and saw there was no breeze. He wet a finger and moistened the notch at the end of the barrel. He took aim at the scout by resting the rifle on his saddled horse. He raised the attached gun sight as high as it would go. He looked for a long time. The scout just stood there, looking for Tom.

He'd missed him entirely.

Tom cocked the rifle and fired.

The sound caught up to the scout in enough time for the bullet to catch him right in his eye socket. Tom saw a red spray fly out of the back of the scout's head. Nodding, Tom quickly removed the sight and repacked the rifle.

The shot would have been heard by the rest of them, so Tom had to hurry to keep the element of surprise in his favor. He jumped back on the horse and took the long way around to where the scout had seen him.

He couldn't risk making any more shots at this point. He hoped they'd send some folks to check on the scout and he'd be able to take care of them quietly. He didn't know what he was riding into, but they didn't know who was riding into them either. That was enough to get them to panic when they found the scout and that's when Tom would take them out.

He hoped.

***

Kicking Fox heard the gunshot even over the screams of Brady, which were formidable. He yelled something in Kiowa and walked over to five of the tribesmen. He gave orders and they left. Cobb watched carefully as they five men left quietly on foot. Brady screamed anew.

There were two men, carefully slicing the skin off of Brady. Half of his torso was covered in rivers of blood as he squirmed violently against the ropes that bound him. He begged them to stop at first, and then just screams.

"Hang in there, son." Cobb said, trying to sound reassuring, but failing. "Helps coming,"

Brady either didn't hear or didn't care.

Kicking Fox came over with a small sack. He reached inside and pulled out a handful of something white. He threw it onto Brady's exposed torso. Brady screamed so hard, Cobb heard his voice box rupture. He passed out after a moment and his head hung down.

He said something to the two torturers. They wiped their knives and went to Cobb striping his clothes in the same way they had done to Brady.

"I feel you're being left out," Kicking Fox said. "If your Rangers are coming, my men will lead them here to see you being skinned."

"If they're coming," Cobb said. "You'll never live long enough to see me die."

"That is fine. I am ready to die. With honor, finally."

"If you stop now, I can make sure you get a fair trial. Go out with a little damn honor."

"You whites know *nothing* of honor," Kicking Fox snarled. "You're invaders. A plague upon the earth. You know nothing of honor. I will die with honor for at least trying to rid the world of you. And I will die smiling with your screams in my ear."

Cobb spit in Kicking Fox's face.

"Figured I'd live up to that whole Spittin' Snake name before you started peelin' me up."

Kicking Fox laughed.

He said something in Kiowa and walked away as Cobb began to scream.

***

The five Kiowa men carefully walked to where their scout, Little Boulder had been told to watch. The saw the spray of blood first and followed it to the body. The shot had completely blown out the back of his head. The look on his face, under the blood was one of surprise.

Standing Tree nodded.

"White Eagle," he said and they all agreed.

"We need to be careful," said Angry Cloud. "He can kill us all without any of us seeing him."

They all looked around.

"He may be behind us already," Standing Tree said.

"We would hear him if he were," said Angry Cloud. "He is not of our people. No white is that clever."

Angry Cloud didn't hear the rock being thrown and didn't feel it slam into the side of his head. He dropped like the stone that had stuck him. The other four men looked around quickly, guns drawn.

Another rock flew into the face of Standing Tree, breaking his nose. He dropped his gun and cried out in pain.

"Where is he?" said Mountain Bear. "We should hear him in the leaves at least."

An arrow struck Mountain Bear through the top of his head. He stood for a moment and waivered before falling. The last two men looked up to see Tom, drawing his knife and jumping down. He buried the knife into the top of the taller one's head while his legs kicked the other in the face. Tom left the knife buried in the dead man's head and rolled over to face the other, who was also coiled and ready to fight.

The Kiowa said something in his native tongue and showed his teeth.

Tom said nothing and pulled out his gun. He shot the Kiowa right in the face.

The Kiowa fell backwards and landed hard. Tom holstered his gun and walked to the brave who had his knife still in his skull. He yanked it out and wiped the blood on his trousers. He went to Angry Cloud first and sliced his throat, letting him bleed out. Then, he turned his attention to Standing Tree. He doubted he'd get any information from him, but it was worth a try.

Standing Tree was writhing, holding his nose. Tom kicked him onto his back and stared at him hard.

"Where are they?" he said through his teeth.

His response was silence.

Tom asked again in Kiowa, surprising Standing Tree.

"You know that I will not tell you, White Eagle." He said. "You will have to find your death by yourself."

"How many of you are left?" Tom asked.

"Too many for you."

"I just killed all five of you," Tom said. "I don't think it matters much anyway."

"I still live."

Tom took his knife and stabbed Standing Tree through the eye.

"And now, you don't." Tom said, wiping the knife on his trousers.

He could still hear Cobb screaming; he'd heard it since climbing the tree and he wanted to get there as quickly as possible, but he couldn't ruin the element of surprise still. He'd get close enough to get a count if possible. If not, he'd take as many down as he could. He'd reload his gun on the way.

If they saw him coming it wouldn't matter.

They were all going to die today. One way or the other.

***

Brady had come to and immediately tried screaming along with Cobb, but it came out in coarse sounding grunts. Two men were working on the two Rangers and they were working faster than earlier. There was an effort now instead of the earlier leisurely way. Four men flanked Kicking Fox who watched the gruesome flaying of the two Texas Rangers. There was a broad smile on his face.

"How is your death coming, Spitting Snake?" He asked.

"Fry in hell," Cobb managed before screaming again. His entire torso and his right leg were skinned completely. He had managed to stay awake the whole time. He wanted to see Kicking Fox get what was coming to him. He wanted to see him dead. And hopefully soon.

"I'm sure, you'll be frying in your own white hell," Kicking Fox said. "Just not as soon as you want."

Kicking Fox and his men chuckled.

There were two gunshots fired simultaneously. The two braves skinning Cobb and Brady fell, bleeding from the backs of their heads. They dropped to their knees and fell over dead.

Kicking Fox whirled around first and saw Tom Wall, a gun in each hand. He fired them both again, killing the two closest braves who still hadn't fully turned around. Kicking Fox reached for his knife and threw himself to the ground. That left one brave, who pulled his gun and fired two shots, both missing Tom entirely. Tom threw one of the guns at the brave who ducked. Tom took three fast steps forward and shot the man twice in the chest. He fell dead.

That left Kicking Fox.

"White Eagle," Kicking Fox said.

Tom nodded, regarding Kicking Fox with the cruel, dead looking eyes for which he had become known. Tom walked towards Kicking Fox.

"As you can see you are already too late. Your white friends are already dead where they stand. And now, you must face me. Are you man enough to face the wrath of-"

Tom shot him between the eyes. Kicking Fox fell backwards and was dead before he hit the ground. Tom didn't break stride as he stepped over Kicking Fox's body, pausing to spit in his face.

He went to Cobb and Brady quickly.

They both looked bad. Brady, wasn't doing anything except twitching. Cobb was breathing heavily and moaning.

"Tom? That you?" Cobb croaked.

"Yes sir," Tom said going to him. "I'm gonna cut you down."

"No son, don't bother." Cobb said. "I seen you kill that son of a bitch. I'm good."

"No, sir, I gotta get you off of this thing. You and Brady."

"Brady's all but dead and I ain't too far behind. Besides, there ain't much living I want to do after this."

Tom didn't know what to do.

"I can save you," Tom said. "I can get the Doc. I just need to go get-"

"The hardest lesson Tom, is you can't save everyone." Cobb said slowly and without much conviction.

"But..." Tom started. "I gotta save you sir."

"I lived a good life. I done everything I needed to do."

"But, you saved *me*," Tom choked out. "I gotta save you."

"Son," Cobb said, smiling. "You saved me a long time ago."

A tear streamed down Tom's face.

"You didn't deserve all the bad that's happened to you, Tom. I hope one day you'll see there's good things in this world too. Cause I think you're one of those good things."

Cobb looked up and smiled as best he could at Tom, whose eyes were red and his face contorted.

"By God, Tom," Cobb said quietly. "I hope you know how damn proud of you I am."

Cobb's head slowly slumped and he died, hanging off of wagon wheel.

Tom, who hadn't cried since the death of his mother dropped to his knees and wept bitterly.

***

Tom waited impatiently outside of Major Hiram Billings' office. He'd been called in after the funeral for both Brady and Cobb; both of which were given heroes funerals. Tom was not in the mood to talk to Major Billings or anybody else for that matter. All he wanted to do was get back to work.

"Come in here, lieutenant." Billings' voice boomed through the door.

Tom opened the door and walked inside.

The office was spacious and covered with awards, pictures and books. Tom doubted he'd read any of the books and decided when he retired, he'd buy books and actually give them a read. Something else to thank Cobb for, he thought.

"You called for me sir?" Tom asked.

"Sit down, Wall." Billings said. He was a big beefy man that Tom couldn't believe was once one of the most famous Texas Rangers who'd ever lived thus far. He'd been one of Cobb's oldest friends at one point.

Tom sat down and looked at Billings.

"Wall, I know you don't want to be here and I don't blame you a bit." Billings said. "But, I been friends with Val Cobb for over thirty years. He didn't have much in the way of a will, but he did leave something behind in case anything ever happened to him. Wanted me to handle it instead of the lawyers. Hot damn, he hated lawyers."

This made Tom smile a little bit.

"Anyway, he left you pretty much everything he had. You was still living in his house?"

Tom nodded.

"Well, it's your house now. He had some money saved up. That's yours too. You can read this thing if you want; idea is, pretty much whatever he had, is yours."

Billings took the official looking papers and laid them in front of Tom on the edge of his desk.

"Is that all, sir?" Tom asked.

"One more thing," Billings said. This time, he stood up and waddled around the desk. "Gonna need you to stand up, Lieutenant."

Confused, Tom stood up.

"At attention, Wall."

Wall stood sharp, the way he'd been taught.

"Upon the recommendation of Captain Valerian T Cobb recently deceased and decorated officer of the Texas Rangers, I hereby promote Lieutenant Tom Wall to the rank of Captain."

Billings reached out and handed Tom a badge made of silver and gold. Tom looked at it.

It was Cobb's badge.

"I didn't have the heart to put it in the pine box with him. I figured you ought to have it."

Tom looked at it for a long time.

"Didn't he have any kin?"

"He sure did, Captain." Billings said, smiling. "And he was damn proud of you too."

CHAPTER 3

Arizona Territory, 1882

Clem smiled as the bullet slammed into his forehead and threw him backward onto the dusty street. When he hit the ground, the dirt and sand flew up around his body. There was a thud and then silence as the dust began to blow in the wind. Blood poured from the hole in Clem's forehead like a geyser. His body gave a small twitch in the bright Arizona sunlight.

Tom Wall holstered his gun and walked toward Clem's body. The sound of his boots broke the silence and the small crowd that had watched quietly began to scatter. It was the way of things; people gunned down in the street for money or justice or both. The show at this point was over and no one had seen anything worth waiting around for anymore.

Wall reached Clem's body and knelt down to look at him. Clem's eyes were still open and he still wore that stupid smile. Wall reached over and closed the dead man's eye lids. He couldn't stand to have him looking up at the sky. He stood up and looked around. Of course there was only the mortician, ready to claim his prize and already moving to take the body with his huge assistant. They were both dressed in black suits and covered in dust.

"That was a hell of a shot, Mr. Wall. Name's Dooley," the mortician said, sticking his hand out. Wall took it and shook quickly. "Yes sir, we heard you'd be looking for Clem and we heard you was a hell of a shot."

"More lucky than anything," Wall said. "How long you reckon you're gonna prop him up for Mr. Dooley?" The mortician shrugged.

"I guess a day or two unless you need to leave in a hurry," Dooley replied. "We got a nice hotel right there across the street and some good eats right next to it."

Wall looked down at Clem. He would clear five hundred dollars after he dragged Clem back to Texas. After tracking him for three months, it was over. Maybe he'd stay a day or two. Maybe he'd earned some sleep in a real bed.

He looked at Dooley, who seemed to be waiting for an answer.

"I reckon a day or two would be good. He's yours until I come for him."

Dooley beamed.

"Oh, thank you Mr. Wall!" he said. He hit the large brute in the ill-fitting suit next to him. "Shake the shit out of your eyes and pick 'em up, Big Pink."

The man he called Big Pink walked over to Clem and grabbed him under his arms. He lifted the big man easily and dragged him away. Dooley had started making light conversation about putting Clem's body on display and money, but Wall had already tuned him out and looked at the hotel. He was suddenly very tired and wanted a drink, and to go to sleep.

He walked away from Dooley, giving a small wave so as not to be rude. He walked slowly to the wooden steps and climbed them as if he had suddenly gained weight.

He opened the door and stepped into the lobby. There were scattered few people sitting, chatting up whores from the place next door, but he ignored them and walked to the front desk. A small burly man walked over to greet him smiling.

"It's an honor to meet you, Mr. Wall," the man said. "I'm Stanley Bosen and I'm the manager here at the Bosen Hotel. I'm sure once the whores next door find out you're staying here, they'll be all over you."

"If you could kind of keep that quiet, I'd be obliged," Wall said. "And you don't have to keep calling me mister. Tom or Wall will do just fine. How much for two nights?"

Bosen smiled.

"Our regular rooms are five a night Mr... I mean, Tom. The suites come with a full bath. Just filled them up about an hour ago. Those are seven fifty. But..." Bosen stopped and grabbed his ledger. "I may be able to make a slight deal with you."

"What kind of 'slight deal?'" Wall asked.

"Well, it seems the object of your visit to our fine little town had stayed here and actually paid for a suite in advance. Three days left to go seein' as he won't be coming back anytime soon." He gave Wall a wink. "It's all yours if you want it. It's a suite!"

Wall considered this. He wasn't broke, not even close, but if he could save a little on the trip…well, maybe he could get a train ticket back to Texas instead of hauling Clem around for weeks. And damn, he was tired.

"I couldn't just stay for free," Wall said. "But a discount would be awful nice."

Bosen smiled even bigger.

"Two dollars a night," Bosen said "And a picture of you to hang up at my billiards room next door. It isn't often we get a genuine celebrity here." Wall frowned.

"I ain't nobody," Wall said. "But I'll take the deal."

"Oh, but you are somebody, Tom. I can try to keep your presence here quiet as I can, but everyone knows who you are and this is the only hotel in town." Bosen said "And that'll be two dollars for the first night."

Wall reached into his pants and pulled out the money requested. Bosen took the money, put it in a drawer and filled out his ledger. He spun the big book around for Wall to sign.

"Just sign here, Tom." Bosen said. Tom grabbed a pen and signed his name. Bosen suddenly slammed the book closed and rang a bell. He pulled a key out from behind the counter and handed it to Wall.

"Your room is 311, top floor. If you wouldn't mind, we'd like to give the room a good once over before you go in and get settled. Take this over to the billiards room next door and have a drink on me."

Bosen handed Wall a round-looking coin that said "FREE DRINK TO THE BARER." He turned it over and it said the same thing.

"We'll let you know when your room is ready, Tom."

Wall nodded and said "Much obliged again." He tipped his hat and walked out of the hotel. As he left, a young man ran over to Bosen at the front desk.

"Please prepare 311 for a new guest. Box up Mr. Clem's items and bring them to me in my office, okay?"

The young man grabbed a ring of keys and ran up the stairs in the center of the room to do as he had been told. Bosen watched Wall through the window slumping over to the billiards room next door. He smiled.

***

Wall knew the second he walked into the billiards room it was a huge mistake. He didn't care though. A free drink was a free drink and he needed one badly.

He tried to keep his head down and walked to a dark corner of the bar. An old bartender came over with a slight limp and a mouth full of bad teeth.

"What can I do you for?" he asked, wiping the dusty bar in front of Wall with a filthy rag.

"You got beer?" Wall asked.

"Hell son, it's even cold." The bartender said, grinning. "That's a quarter if you want it."

Wall slapped the drink token on the bar and slid it to the bartender.

"Well then, a drink for our special guest," the bartender said. "On the house at that!" The bartender disappeared and returned with a foamy mug of beer. He set it in front of Wall, who grabbed it and downed about half of it before putting it down again.

"God damn, that's cold!" he said, laughing a little. He wiped his mouth off on his sleeve and smiled. How long had it been since he smiled? He couldn't recall. The bartender laughed with him.

"Told you son, we serve 'em cold here."

"Damned if you don't," Wall said. He reached into his pocket and pulled out some coins. He put four on the bar.

"That first one's on the house, but keep them coming, sir." Wall said, reaching for his beer.

"Call me Hank, and you got it. Don't drink 'em all that fast. Your head'll feel like old Clem's before too long if you do."

Wall laughed again and took a deep drink of the beer. He had always been amazed at how one small thing could turn you right around. He was ready to go lie down and he was still damn tired, but a cold beer was a rare thing even in the big cities. And just when he needed a cold drink, he found it in the tiny town of...of...

"Hank, what's the name of this town?" Wall asked, but Hank had gone on to help another customer.

Aw, hell with it. Who cares? Wall thought. Just enjoy your damn drink, dummy.

He adjusted how he was sitting and began to relax for the first time in weeks. He took a deep breath and let it out slowly. He closed his eyes for a minute and let the cold fire in his belly soothe him a little bit.

It didn't last long.

He felt a hand gently touch his shoulder. His nose was filled with flowers and almonds. The hand gently massaged his shoulder and moved down to his back.

A whore.

He opened his eyes and expected to see a large woman, rode hard for too many years and looking to make some money. What he saw was something he'd not expected.

She was beautiful. Couldn't have been more than twenty if that; she had coral lips, grey eyes and a mop of long curly black hair that was tied in an unruly bun underneath a small hat. She was dressed like a fine lady. He knew damn well she wasn't, but she could pass for one to be sure. She saw him looking at her and she smiled.

"Hello, Mr. Wall. Buy a lady a drink?"

Wall honestly didn't know what to say, so he smiled. He brushed the seat next to him off and gestured for her to sit. He forgot his manners, but recovered enough to stand slightly until she sat. She winked at him.

"You are definitely not from anywhere near here are you? Such courtesy." She said smiling. Wall blushed a little. Must be the beer, he thought. He slapped his hand on the bar and beckoned Hank over, who obliged.

"Drink for the lady and I'll take another beer please," Wall said. He looked at the girl, who gave a shy nod, still smiling.

"I'll get you and Veronique drinks right quick. And, good call son!" Hank went to get the drinks and Veronique turned to Wall.

"Thank you," she said. "And might I say, that was one hell of a shot you made on Mr. Jackson a little while ago. Hell of a shot."

"Thanks," was all Wall could think to say. He picked up the rest of his beer and downed it in one gulp. It felt good and he was feeling a little loose. He had to be careful not to get too loose; Veronique was a whore and as pretty as she was, just a whore out for some of his money. He'd known enough whores that would slit your neck if you had enough money on you.

She didn't seem the type, but he'd been wrong about women before.

"Where did you learn to shoot like that?" she asked.

"Ma'am, I was a Texas Ranger for about ten years. Learned real quick you had better hit what you're shooting at, or you wouldn't last too long in the job."

Her eyes lit up.

"A real Texas Ranger? That's exciting!" Veronique pulled a little book out of the side of her dress. It was a penny dreadful that had a picture of what was supposed to be Wall. She held it up.

"I must have read this about twenty times and it didn't say anything about you being a Texas Ranger." She said. Wall frowned and took the little book.

The title of the dreadful was "Tom Wall: Youngest and Best Bounty Hunter This Side of the Pecos River! Becoming a Legend before Thirty!"

Quick Draw Killer!

Wall looked at it for a while and then laughed. He handed it back to Veronique.

"Well, I reckon they got my age right, but they probably got just about everything else wrong," He said as Hank dropped off their drinks. Wall pushed the money over the bar, but Hank waved his hand.

"I started you a tab, son. Go get yourself in some trouble there. I got other people that need drinks." He winked and left.

He grabbed his beer and she reached for her drink; a glass of wine of some kind. She held it up.

"Cheers, Mr. Wall. Here's to us."

He clinked his beer as gently as he could to her wine glass.

"To...us." He said.

The two took a few sips of their drinks and began to talk to each other. He was learning a lot about himself; that was one thing. She must've read that damn penny dreadful a lot more than twenty times; she was quoting entire passages verbatim from the book. Although the stories she was asking him about were pure made up bullshit, it was pretty flattering to hear someone talk to him about him for a change. He watched her as she lit up, talking about his alleged adventures and watching her sink and then laugh as he told the real version.

He also knew when he was being played and he wasn't getting that feeling from Veronique. Maybe it was the beer. Maybe it wasn't, but he was enjoying himself.

Relaxing.

He felt good.

After a few more cold beers and wine, they decided to get something to eat. They asked Hank about the food and he assured them he'd have something nice fixed up for them. In a short while, he brought out two steaming wooden bowls of stew and some crusty bread. Veronique took little bites, but Wall devoured his after the first bite.

"Hank, what kind of meat is this?" Wall asked, with a mouthful of the stew.

"Fresh," Hank replied. "Good ain't it? The wife does a damn good job, don't you think?"

Wall smiled and nodded as he tore back into the bowl. He was finished in five minutes. Veronique giggled as he looked up at her, mouth covered with stew.

"Lord, excuse me," He said and laughed a little himself. "Been so long since I had a sit down meal, I forgot my manners."

"I like to see a man eat," Veronique said, grabbing a napkin from the bar and wiping his mouth. She leaned in closer to him and said "What else has it been a long time for, Mr. Wall?"

***

Veronique lay sleeping with an arm across Wall's chest. He looked down at her and smiled to himself. They came to his room, took a bath together and spent the next few hours exhausting and pleasing each other. He'd been with his share of whores, but she seemed less like one and more like someone he could be with for a long time. It was a fool's thought to be sure, but he was enjoying all of her, even while she slept.

He had tried to sleep along with her, but he was wide awake. The combination of the beer, food and sex should have knocked him out and he knew this, but he was up and alert. He kept looking at her and stroked her hair. She gave a little smile in her sleep and he felt her snuggle up closer to him.

"I could get used to this," he whispered. Veronique opened her eyes and looked up at him.

"Why Mr. Wall," she said in her own whisper. "You sound a little bit smitten."

Wall had to laugh and she climbed on top of him and kissed his cheek.

"I reckon I ain't alone in it either," he said kissing her neck.

"No sir, you are not." She said, finding his mouth. They kissed deep and hard for a moment until she broke off and looked at him.

"You don't always kiss whores like that, do you Mr. Wall?"

"No I do not," he said. "But I ain't really thinking of you as a whore. And, it's Tom. Not mister anything to you."

A small tear streamed down her face and she kissed him again. He reached up and grabbed her as they fell into each other again. When they finished this time, he fell asleep tangled in Veronique's arms and he slept as well as he ever did.

***

Wall awoke to find the room dark. Veronique was still sleeping next to him and he carefully got out of the bed. Naked, he walked over to the heavy oak dresser where he'd thrown most of what was in his pockets and found his matches. He lit the oil lamp on the dresser and looked for his pocket watch. He popped it open and saw through the dim light that the watch had stopped. He frowned, but realized he didn't really care about the time, but he had started to think about dragging Clem's body back to Texas.

He looked at Veronique, sleeping peacefully on the bed. What was he going to do about her? It hurt his head to think about leaving her here, but could he haul her and a stinking corpse on a train bound for Texas? He sure as hell couldn't take her on the trail if he decided to go that way.

He decided he needed some air, so he quietly put on his dungarees, boots, a shirt and strapped his gun on just in case. He left the room quietly and walked down the dimly lit hallway toward the stairs. As he walked slowly down the carpeted staircase, he heard voices speaking in hushed tones. He resisted the urge to stop and listen as was ingrained in him from a decade in the Texas Rangers. It was harder than he thought it would be, and his hand found itself resting on his gun anyway.

That urge, he never resisted.

When he finished his descent, he saw Bosen and Dooley, the mortician chatting away quietly. They both regarded him and smiled.

"Nice night for a walk, Mr. Wall?" Bosen asked, smiling.

Wall walked closer to the two men. Dooley looked as pale as milk.

"Feeling a little poorly, Mr. Dooley?" Wall asked.

Dooley swallowed and shook his head.

"I'm...yes. Poorly, that's about right." His voice sounded shaky. "We're gonna prop your bounty in front of the hotel in the morning, Mr. Wall. If you'd like to pose for some of those pictures, that would sure help things along."

Wall shook his head.

"You do what you need to do with him, but I've already done what I needed to do with that bastard. Save for draggin' him back to Texas that is."

Dooley nodded.

"When do you reckon you'll be heading back?" Dooley asked.

"I ain't sure just yet. I'll let you know before the end of tomorrow. Depends on the train schedule."

"Train?" Dooley turned paler if that were possible. "You gonna put him on a train?"

"If I had wings, I'd fly that crooked son of a bitch back to Texas." Wall said, flatly. "I don't want to have to spend any more time with him than I have to. I spent three months chasing his ass here. I'm done." Bosen laughed.

"Well, you should take your time to decide, Mr. Wall. Still have a few days on that room after all. Besides, Mr. Dooley can put him on ice so he doesn't stink up the train when you leave at the end of the week if that's what you decide to do."

Bosen leaned over the counter.

"And I'm sure your new 'friend' would sure like you to stay a little longer."

Wall nodded.

"I'll think about it," was all he said. He tipped his hat and walked out the hotel door. Dooley followed right behind him.

As he walked along the street, he felt a little chilly, but it also felt good. He still had the lingering smell of Veronique on him and he again thought about getting used to it.

"What do you want Mr. Dooley?" Wall asked the man behind him. He kept walking and the mortician followed behind him.

"I wanted to talk to you Mr. Wall. Can you stop for a minute?" "I can walk and talk at the same time if it's all the same to you." Dooley sighed, but walked faster to catch up to Wall's longer stride.

"I was wondering," Dooley began. "If you had thought about leaving a little sooner."

Wall said nothing.

"You know, to get a jump on the trip? Get home earlier? Relax before your next job?"

"This here is my last job," Wall replied. "And I'm relaxing just fine." Wall stopped and whirled to look at Dooley.

"Some reason I should leave?" he asked a trifle cold.

Dooley stopped dead in his tracks. He looked terrified, but not of Wall.

"Well, sir, I really can't…I'm not at liberty to…oh my," Dooley was shaking all over. "I can't do this anymore,"

"Do what?" Wall was genuinely confused. "What are you going on about, Dooley? You're as white as a sheet."

Dooley grabbed a wooden column and held himself up.

"It's too much," he said, nearly sobbing. "Just too damned much. It's got to end."

Wall moved toward Dooley and held a hand out to steady the man, but Dooley moved away from him.

"This town is poison, Mr. Wall. The longer you stay, the harder it'll be for you to leave and leave you must!"

"What do you mean poison?"

He thought of Veronique and wondered why the hell he got out of bed.

"I mean poison. This place, this damn town is a trap!" Dooley was tearing up and drooling slightly.

"You're talkin' shit, Dooley."

Dooley grabbed Wall's arm and pulled him close.

"Come with me quickly" he said and began to drag Wall down the street.

***

They arrived a few minutes later at a barn that had a sign on the front. "Arthur P. Dooley: Mortician and Undertaker. Do Not Enter!" Although it was dark, the big white lettering was pretty easy to read in moonlight. Dooley fumbled with a key and unlocked the barn door. He unengaged the lock and looked at Wall, who looked confused.

"Do you have matches?" Dooley asked.

Wall held up his small tinderbox and nodded.

"Come inside, quick." Dooley said and disappeared into the barn. Wall hesitated a moment and looked around. He had no idea why someone would follow him here, but he'd been a ranger too long to act otherwise.

He carefully walked into the barn.

Dooley waited until he was in all the way and closed the door.

"Come here with your matches," Dooley said and walked quickly over to a large heavy blanket covering up something large. On a small table next to it was an oil lamp. He reached out for the tinderbox and Wall handed it to him. Dooley's hand was shaking so badly, he couldn't strike the match.

Wall, not needing to be asked, walked over and took the matches away to light the lamp.

"Thank you," Dooley said quietly.

Wall lit the match and touched it to the wick. He put the glass cover on it and turned the wick up about an inch for maximum light. He was a few feet from the covered object and felt cold.

"This is where I keep the bodies when they aren't on display," Dooley explained. "The blanket slows down the melting a little and it also covers up the box and the smell. You may want to hold your nose or something."

"I've smelled worse," Wall said but braced himself anyway. Dooley Pulled the blanket off and there between the two ice blocks was a wooden coffin with the lid off. Inside was Clem, still smiling and the bullet hole in his forehead, looking like a third eye.

The body was stripped naked to the pants, but there was something not right.

Most of his torso was missing.

Wall moved closer to look and the smell indeed was awful, but it didn't stop him. He turned and grabbed the oil lamp from the small table carefully.

"Careful, Mr. Wall." Dooley said.

"I ain't an idjit," Wall said calmly. "Just want to see what the hell this is all about."

He moved the lamp closer and saw that almost the entire torso was picked damn near clean. There was almost no blood, as if the body had never had any inside.

"So why would you do this, Mr. Dooley? There ain't nothing but a set of ribs left, This some kind of undertaker thing?"

"I didn't do this," Dooley said. "My young associate Big Pink did this and he was told to do it. This is why you need to leave." Wall frowned.

"What the hell do I tell them folks when I go to claim my bounty on this man?" Wall was getting angry.

Dooley shook his head.

"You're missing the point, Mr. Wall."

Wall stepped backward and put the lamp down. He looked at Dooley.

"You're telling me I need to leave right now for no good god damn reason and then you show me that you desecrated this dumb bastard's corpse and expect me to haul it back like this?"

"This is what happens to folks who die here, Mr. Wall. This is what always happens to them."

"What, somebody dies and they scoop 'em out like a damn canoe? That don't make no sense at all."

"Do you want to know why he was smiling when you shot him?"

"I just told you he was a dumb bastard," Wall replied.

"No, no. Think back to before you shot him. What did he say?"

Wall thought about it. He didn't like to think about the act of killing, especially folks he'd killed; whether they deserved it or not. It was still taking a life and although Clem's life wasn't worth shit, it was still a life.

Wall had been walking up the street when Clem had come running out of the bar attached to the hotel.

"Clem Jackson!" Wall had yelled and the stupid son of a bitch stopped dead in his tracks. He looked at Wall for a long time.

"Come all this way to fetch me Tommy?" Clem asked, snickering. "All this was just for me?"

"I can bring you in one of two ways, Clem." Wall said. "I'd be obliged if you were able to walk to your hanging."

"What's the difference if I'm already a dead man?"

"A hundred dollars," Wall said flatly and Clem laughed.

"Well, damn your hundred dollars. You're going to have to kill me."

"I'd rather not," Wall said. "I'll see you get a fair trial."

"Trust me Tommy," Clem said, moving toward Wall. "If you kill me know, you'll be doing me a favor."

Wall pulled his gun and aimed it at Clem.

"Not another step." He said.

Clem smiled and kept walking.

"Oh, I'll take all the steps I can get if you're gonna put me down. And that's what everybody wants." Wall shook his head.

"Clem? You best stop coming now, I ain't foolin'." He continued forward.

"Just do it," Clem said, smiling. "I got it comin' and I want it. I want it *now*!"

Clem pretended to reach for his gun and Wall shot him right between the eyes.

The smile never left his face as he fell. As he fell, Wall had noticed that he wasn't wearing a side holster. He'd shot him unarmed. Normally that would have bothered him, but Clem did in fact have it coming after all.

Wall looked at Dooley.

"He said 'You'd be doing me a favor.'" Dooley said and the words that had been lost on Wall suddenly has some weight.

"How long had Clem been here before I found him?" Wall asked.

"About two days," Dooley said after a pause. "He was living it up the first night. Whores, liquor, the food and the works. All poison." Dooley wiped his palms on his suit. "He didn't want to leave until it was too late. He tried to, but he couldn't. And then you showed up." Wall sighed.

"Sounds like he was having a good time. Why would he want to leave?"

"Exactly," Dooley said. "That's what you need to ask yourself. Why would he want to leave?"

Wall was missing something and he hated missing something. He told this to Dooley. Dooley responded with a question.

"You see any livestock on your way into this town?"

"No I didn't. I figured you had a delivery here and there what with all this ice to keep it cool-"

"Where's all this ice coming from?" Dooley asked. His eyes narrowed. "Where's a dog? Or a horse? Or a god damn fly? For that matter, where's your horse?"

Wall's horse was dead, he knew that much, but that was about it. He couldn't think of a reason for any of the questions, but just because he couldn't think of one, didn't mean there wasn't one.

"Mr. Dooley, I think I'm done here. I'll be leaving in the morning with my claim. I'd appreciate it if you could write something up explaining why his god damn innards are missing." Wall turned and walked to the barn door.

Dooley hurried after him.

"But you have to leave now!" Dooley cried. "Don't you see? It'll be too late in the morning!"

Wall turned and grabbed Dooley by the jacket.

"I've about had enough of this, Dooley. You talk in circles and you desecrate the dead. If I were still a Texas Ranger, I'd haul you back with Clem and have you strung up for good measure."

"This isn't Texas," Dooley said. "You'd have no jurisdiction here." Wall jerked the man up to his face.

"My jurisdiction is wherever I happen to be." With that, he pushed Dooley back and kicked the barn door open. "Have him ready to travel. I'll come for him in the morning."

***

By the time Wall walked back into the hotel, the place was dark and quiet. There was some noise coming from the billiards room next door, but that was to be expected. He had noticed that he couldn't hear a single cricket on his walk back to the hotel and was going to ask Veronique when he got back upstairs.

He climbed the stairs two at a time and a little faster as he thought about Veronique. Right now, all he wanted was her. He gave a little distracted laugh and marveled at how often he'd smiled and laughed since he pulled into this town.

It was her.

He decided he was going to ask her to come with him.

Wall reached the top of the stairs and turned right down the hall to his room. He got to the door and pulled his boots off to try and be quiet in case she was still sleeping. He heard her before opening the door and she was crying. He threw the door open, dropped his boots and drew his gun.

He saw her wide eyed and sitting on the bed, still naked. She recoiled from Wall as he looked around the room.

"You all right?" He asked sternly. She gave a little yelp and stared at him. "Is somebody in here?"

She shook her head slowly 'no' and began to cry again. Wall holstered his gun and ran to the bed.

"What's wrong darlin'? I thought someone was in here with you hurtin' you or somethin'."

She lunged into his arms.

"I thought you left me," she said through a hail of sobs. She clutched him tightly. "I know it's stupid because I'm just a whore and all, but..." He grabbed her back and chuckled.

"I ain't leavin' you," he said. "And you just made askin' you to come with me a hell of a lot easier."

She hugged him tighter and then kissed his neck. She looked up at him.

"Oh Tom, I love you." She said, still crying, a serious look on her face. "But I can't leave."

Wall looked down at her.

"What do you mean, can't leave?"

She sniffed.

"Darling, we can't ever leave here if we're gonna be together. We just can't."

Wall kissed her head and stood up.

"What are you scared of? Of course we can leave. Anytime we want." She pulled a blanket around her and stood up.

"You don't understand. I have to stay here. You can go, but I have to stay."

Wall folded his arms.

"Is it Bosen? You work for him, right? What's it gonna take to get you out of here?"

She shook her head.

"It's more than just that," she said. "A lot more. It's this town, Tom. It's..."

"Poison?"

She looked shocked.

"Who told you that?"

"Dooley. Just showed me a thing or two." He walked over to the dresser and turned the fading oil lamp up a little for more light. He started to gather his things.

"Like, Clem Jackson, with a lot of his insides gone. He was trying to get me to leave before sunrise. Said the town was poison."

Veronique walked over to him.

"It *is* poison, Tom and it won't matter if it's sunrise or not." She put a hand on his shoulder. "I want you to stay but only if you love me." He turned and looked at her. He kissed her forehead.

"I do love you, which is why we're both gettin' the hell out of this place. What do you want to bring with you?"

She gave a sob and a sigh.

"Tom, you don't understand. I can't leave."

Wall took the bed roll and threw it down. He grabbed Veronique and brought her closer to his face.

"I'm getting awful tired of being talked to in circles. What the hell is the problem?"

As she recoiled from him, the door flew open. Wall snapped his head in the door's direction and saw Bosen, holding a shotgun aimed right at the two of them.

"The lady said, she can't leave and she can't, Mr. Wall." Bosen said, smiling a little. "You'd do well to let her loose now."

He looked at her and let her go. She backed away from him slowly, turning to Bosen.

"Don't hurt him, Stanley. He loves me."

Bosen laughed.

"That's because he doesn't know you very well."

Wall frowned.

"Now just a damn minute, Bosen!"

Bosen raised the shotgun and moved closer to Wall.

"You hold on a minute, son." Bosen said. "We were gonna let you ride on out of here, but you're making it awful hard for me to not blow your head off. There's a lot at work here, Mr. Wall."

Wall counted to himself all the way to three before Bosen's shotgun was close enough. He grabbed the barrel, yanked it hard to one side and pulled it right out of Bosen's hands. Wall wrapped both hands around the barrel and drove the wooden handle by the trigger into Bosen's forehead, knocking him down. Wall flipped the gun and cocked it, aiming at Bosen, who was now bleeding from his forehead.

"Why don't you start telling me what's at work here before I lose my sunny disposition," Wall said coldly. Bosen looked surprised and then he smiled.

"It's all about to become clear, Mr. Wall." Bosen said, holding his head. Wall was about to respond when a sharp blow turned the dark room darker and Wall fell to the floor, unconscious.

***

Wall woke up and couldn't move. He opened his eyes and saw the ceiling of a barn. It hurt his head to move, but he looked from side to side and saw he'd been tied to a wooden table. His feet and hands were spread out and lashed to the legs of the table and heavy rope tight across his chest.

"Hey!" he yelled out. "You best cut me loose!"

A moment later, the barn door opened and he felt a hot rush of air hit him as sunlight poured into the barn.

"Good morning, Mr. Wall!" Bosen said, walking in slowly. Wall strained to see him and the two figures with him. It was Hank the bartender and Veronique. She moved quickly over to Wall and touched his face. "Tom, I'm so sorry. This is all my fault." It was Wall's turn to recoil from her.

"Why did you hit me?" he asked.

"I couldn't let you kill Stanley," she said sadly. "He's a no good bastard, but you can't just kill him."

Wall struggled with his bonds to no avail. He looked at Veronique in pure anger.

"You said you loved me,"

She smiled sweetly.

"I do, so very much my love." She said and stroked his face. "And I always will."

He struggled again. Veronique looked at him sadly and moved away from him.

Hank leaned closer to Bosen.

"Maybe we shoulda kept Big Pink around a little longer," he said. Bosen shook his head.

"Mr. Wall, do you know where you are?" Wall stopped struggling

"I reckon I'm in Dooley's barn with Clem's body cooling off," he said. Bosen clapped his hands.

"Yes, poor Mr. Dooley. We had to let him and his charge go earlier this morning." Bosen said

"That means," Hank chimed in, "We had them destroyed."

"Enough," Bosen said. "Hank, I want to hear something out of you, I'll god damn ask for it."

Wall swallowed hard.

"You have put us in a rather strange position, Mr. Wall. We can't let you leave, but we don't want to kill you either in spite of your rush to hitting me in the head." Bosen said.

"Cut me loose and I'll do more than hit your head, Bosen." Wall said through his teeth.

Bosen laughed. He walked over to Wall and looked down at him.

"You know what the name Bosen means, Mr. Wall?" Wall didn't answer.

"It's a German word. It means 'evil.' I don't tell you that to scare you or nothing, but it is my name and there are lots of folks that would say it's appropriate."

Wall looked up at him and said nothing.

"You don't scare easy and I like that, Mr. Wall. So I'm going to make a deal with you for the sake of your lover over there. Are you listening?"

Wall nodded.

"Good. Like I said I don't want to kill you, but I will. I don't have the burden of feeling bad or guilty about things I have to do, but I don't like to waste things either." He pointed to a different side of the barn. "Your prize, Clem Jackson over there is a perfect example. Dooley showed what's left of him to you, yes?" Again, Wall nodded.

"Did he happen to tell you why?"

"No he did not."

"Food, Mr. Wall. We used him for food."

Wall allowed this to sink in and struggled to get free again. Bosen waited for him to stop and when he did, he smiled.

"Before you go on and start getting the idea that we're gonna eat you, I want you to consider something. There are a lot of things in this world you don't know or understand. Folks hate what they don't understand. You hate rattlesnakes because if you piss them off, they'll bite and kill you. But they have their purpose. Part of God's plan. Just like us." Wall looked at him with disgust.

"Eating your own kind is part of God's plan? That's bullshit."

Bosen leaned down to Wall's face. He saw that Bosen's eyes weren't any color at all. They were almost all black.

"Consider that Mr. Jackson, was not *our* kind." Bosen said.

"What the hell does that mean?" Wall asked.

Veronique walked over to Wall carefully.

"Tom, please listen. We can still be together," she pleaded.

"Yes," Bosen said, still near Wall's face. "You can still be with her, very much alive and probably pretty happy. But I'm only making this deal once."

Wall looked at Veronique and then back at Bosen, who looked hungry.

"What we are, and by that I mean everyone in this town isn't as important as what we *do*." Bosen stood back, becoming aware of his drooling. "We take the unsavory elements of society and dispose of them. Like Mr. Jackson. We lie in wait for brigands, thieves, murderers and the like to come to our town and we kill them. And then, because of what we are, we eat them. So we don't have to go to a big town and kill innocent people. God's plan."

"We aren't really people," Veronique said shyly. "But we're pretty close...and I do love you so."

Wall looked at Bosen in horror.

"Dooley said this town was poison. Like a trap." Tom said. He understood what the town was now. "You're like god damn *spiders*." he said.

Bosen looked at Veronique and smiled.

"That's a very good analogy! I quite like that, Mr. Wall."

"You're cannibals. Monsters!"

Bosen's smile faded and he got very close to Wall's face again.

"We are *Americans*, sir!" Bosen snarled. "This country has been very good and kind to us. The least we can do is not eat those who have done us no harm."

"When I was a little girl," Veronique began. "My kind were hunted down and slaughtered for what we are. I am the only one in my family still alive." Hank stepped forward.

"It works out, Mr. Wall. Sure, what we do seems gruesome to you. But look what we do. Only criminals. Bad folks, trying to escape the law. We're doing regular folks a favor."

Wall remembered what Clem had said before he shot him in the forehead.

You'll be doing me a favor.

"You see, Mr. Wall. We aren't evil. Just like a spider isn't evil for eating bugs and such." Bosen said.

"People ain't bugs," Wall said, his heart pounding.

"Aren't they?" Veronique asked. "You think Clem Jackson wasn't worse than a bug?"

Wall struggled again and he was no closer to getting free than he was before. He looked up and closed his eyes. He was angry and scared; two things he knew were a bad combination in his predicament. He tried to calm himself down but couldn't.

"Tom, I love you no matter what I am or what you are," Veronique said, moving closer to him. She stroked his face and he didn't bother to move away. He knew he was finished. "What we feel for each other is real. You didn't care that I was a whore. Why should you care now?" With his eyes still closed, Wall spoke.

"Please tell me this is a nightmare. Please tell me you ain't gonna eat me. I can't believe any of this."

She took both of her hands and grabbed his face.

"Look at me Tom. Look at me!"

Wall opened his eyes and looked into her grey eyes. Son of bitch, he thought. I *do* love her. She smiled at him.

"It's still just me."

Bosen stepped closer.

"Here's the deal, Mr. Wall. Stay here with us. Be one of us. Be with Veronique. Help us rid this world of truly bad people."

Wall sniffed and opened his eyes. He looked up at Veronique, who was still smiling at him.

"Or?"

"Or, we kill you and put you in the next batch of Hank's wife's stew." Bosen said flatly. "We didn't want it to go like this, I promise you. We don't want to kill you."

"But we'll damn sure eat ya, son. That's a damn fact." Hank added. Veronique shot him a dirty look and Hank put his hands up. "Hey, I'm just sayin',"

Bosen put a hand on Veronique's shoulder.

"Let's let him think 'bout this," He said to her, but Wall shook his head.

"She can stay," Wall said quietly.

Bosen nodded.

"We'll give you a few minutes." Bosen said and guided Hank out of the barn.

There was a long time that passed as Wall and Veronique looked at each other. Wall spoke first.

"Can you let me go? I'd never come back here, whatever the name of this town is, I'd leave you all be."

Veronique shook her head and smiled.

"No, you wouldn't Tom. It isn't in you to leave something like us. Like me."

Wall sighed.

"I reckon you're right," he said sadly. "Do you...are you...really a monster?"

"I am what I am," she said and bent down to kiss him. He didn't resist and kissed her back. When she pulled back he was smiling.

"If it's gonna be done, I want you to do it, Veronique." Wall said. "I love you, but I can't live like this, knowing what it is you folks do. I couldn't abide by it."

"No, please Tom." she cried.

"If you have any love at all for me, you do it. Do it now!" Wall yelled.

Veronique's body began to shake and Wall watched in horror as to what was happening. Her beautiful porcelain skin began to darken before his eyes and her lovely grey eyes recessed into her skull. The skin on her face seemed to peel back and displayed an odd, exposed skull, nearly ebony in color. Her mouth, her beautiful smile became a jagged maw of sharpened fangs and the thing she was becoming snarled at him. He was terrified beyond belief. He screamed and screamed until everything went black and he felt himself falling

***

The sunlight was the first thing Wall saw when he awoke. He covered his eyes with his arms and turned his head away. He blinked several times and realized he wasn't in the barn. He was on the ground. He rolled over to see where he was.

He was in a patch of sand near a river; he heard it trickling in the background. He felt nauseous and retched to one side. After it passed, he sat up and looked around. There was some shade near a tree and his bedroll was underneath the tree.

He kept looking around as he got to his feet. He looked off into the distance and saw a plume of black smoke. He watched it for a while and walked awkwardly to the tree where his bedroll sat, waiting for him. He sat down and grabbed the roll to open it. Inside were all of his things, the few of them that he had, minus his watch.

Two items were new however; a canteen full of probably water and a letter. He opened the canteen, sniffed it and drank two large gulps. He held up the letter that read simply, "Tom." He knew it was from her.

He tore it open and began to read.

My Dear Tom,

I could not bring myself to kill you. I don't know if you believe me or not, but I do and always will love you. We have burned the town. We have moved on to somewhere you won't find us and please, do not look for us. We aren't bad or evil. You should know that by now.

If they see you coming for us, they will kill you. I won't be able to stop them next time.

I wish we could have been together, my love.

~~*Viorica*~~
Veronique

Wall sat and frowned at the crossed off name. *Was that her real name?* He ignored it for the moment and re read the letter for a good long time until he began to weep.

He put everything back into the bed roll and stood up. He dusted himself off and found that the rope used to tie him to the table in the barn was still tied around his chest. He grabbed it and untied himself from the thick rope. He held it out in front of him. It was a good five feet of rope.

He looked up at the tree where he stood and saw a thick branch. He started to laugh.

He had just enough rope to hang himself and he laughed.

CHAPTER 4

One Year Later-Temperance, Oklahoma

Jud was going to say "Draw."

It was right there on the tip of his tongue, ready to pass through the lips that was just beginning to make the words when the bullet slammed into his chest. He had enough time to make a noise that sounded like he said 'Woof' before falling backwards onto the street. His last thought was of his mother's apple pie as his mouth filled with his own blood.

The two men flanking Jud looked at their hands and raised them over their heads, shaking.

The man opposite them cocked his revolver and pointed it at the man on his left.

"Unhook your gun belts with your left hands and let 'em drop,' He said, then added, "The *other* left, goddamnit."

The men complied quickly. When the belts and guns had dropped, the man said, "Now, kick them guns over and lie down face first. Hands on the back of your heads."

He walked towards the men as they did what he asked. When they were both down, he holstered his gun and stood over them.

"Name's Wall. You two are in my custody. I don't care if you did all the things the State of Tennessee thinks you did, but there's a reward I'm gonna claim with you three. The price is the same dead or alive. Your choice on how you get delivered. As you can see," he kicked Jud in the ribs to make his point. "It's all the same to me."

Ten minutes later, the two men were up, in leg shackles and carrying their now dead partner, Jud. Jud always had a big damn mouth, and the two men were glad he was the dead one.

"Goddamn dummy," said the man called Scar.

"He sure was," said the man called Spoon.

"Shut your yaps," Wall said behind them. "We're going to the undertaker to get him in a box. Ain't no sense in you two hauling him all over hell's creation."

Scar grunted, but Spoon spoke up.

"How are we getting back?" Wall spit.

"Train. You'll be shackled up in the hold with him."

Scar chuckled.

"Ain't never been on no train," he said.

"Better enjoy it," Wall said. "Ain't likely to get another one after this."

This shut both men up and they shuffled to the undertaker's place of business.

When they got to G.I. Suckley's undertaking establishment, Wall had the two men drop the body of Jud on the right side of the porch. He then adjusted the shackle around the left side of the porch's support beam.

"I reckon he smelled that bad before I shot him," Wall said. "Can't get him more down wind. You boys behave." Wall said as he walked through the front door.

The place was poorly lit with candles and smelled of rotten flowers; still sweet but with something else behind it. There was a front desk with a bell, which Wall tapped three times.

After a moment, a tall slender man in a white shirt and an apron came from the back room. There were dark stains on the shirt that didn't take a genius to figure out what they were.

"You Suckley?" Wall asked.

The thin man smiled.

"Yes sir, G. I. Suckley." He stuck out a blood soaked hand and then, thought better of it.

"Sorry," he said. "I've been a bit busy."

"Well, I guess business is good for you then," Wall said. "I have an easy one for you. Just need a box for shipping." Suckley looked confused.

"A box for shipping?"

Wall simply glared at him.

"He's on your porch," Wall said. "Got his two pals chained up next to them. Is that alright?"

"Um…sure, sir. Not a problem…um, so you only need a casket?" Suckley stammered.

"Just a box big enough to fit him suits me. Don't need to be fancy." Suckley nodded.

"Well, let's get him in here. You say you have folks chained to my porch?"

Wall nodded.

"They can bring him in, put him where you need him."

"How would you like the body prepared?"

"Quick as you can. In the box," Wall said and began to walk to the porch.

As he opened the door to the porch, he noticed two things at once. First, the two men were still shackled, but now they were as far left as they could physically go, straining against their chains. Before Wall could ask why, he saw Jud, sitting up and growling in a low voice.

Wall stepped out, drew his gun and moved left, next to the two men.

"When was y'all going to let me know he wasn't dead?" Wall asked, aiming his gun. He didn't get a reply and he looked at the men quickly.

They were petrified.

Wall turned back to Jud who was still trying to stand and still growling.

"Stand down, Jud." Wall said, cocking his gun. "You're hurt bad. I'll get the doc."

Jud looked up at Wall. His growl went to a snarl and Wall looked in his eyes.

Jud's eyes were bloodshot, but bright grey at the same time. He seemed to look right through Wall. Wall had seen a lot of odd things, but this wasn't one of them. He saw the bullet wound in Jud's chest; he never missed. It was a kill shot. He tilted his head and looked at Jud, still staring, still trying to stand.

"Jud, you understand me?"

"Shoot him, Wall, for Christ's sake," Spoon said, nearly in a whisper.

"Stop talking to him."

"Quiet," Wall said, still looking at Jud. "Let's see what he does."

Jud, halfway up, stumbled and fell on his back, like a kid trying to walk for the first time.

At that moment, Suckley came through the front door onto the porch. He saw Jud sprawled out on the porch and went over to him, bending down. Wall opened him mouth to speak when Jud looked up and saw Suckley. Suckley gasped as Jud snarled and grabbed the undertaker by his neck. Suckley fell on top of Jud, as Jud opened his mouth and bit into Suckley's face, tearing off his cheek. Suckley screamed as Wall quickly walked to pull him off.

He grabbed Suckley under his arms and tried to pull him up, but Jud held him tightly by his head.

"Let him up, Jud." Wall said and yanked on Suckley again. Jud, still chewing, opened his mouth for another bite. Suckley drew a deep breath and screamed again.

Wall let Suckley go and drew his gun. He put the barrel right in Jud's mouth and fired. Jud stopped moving and released Suckley, who rolled off of Jud still screaming and holding his cheek. A real good chunk of it was missing and Wall could see the man's teeth.

Spoon and Scar finally found their voices and began to yell the name of Jesus and all the saints.

"Quit your wailin'," Wall snapped and tried to help up Suckley.

"Come on now," he said as he pulled the man up to his feet.

Suckley, who was going into shock, looked at Wall with wide eyes. He tried to speak, but it came out in little gasps and sputters.

"Don't try to speak," Wall said. "Let's get you inside and I'll go find the Doctor."

Suckley nodded slightly and began to cry. Wall put an arm around him and helped him in the door, telling his two prisoners, "Make sure you two open your goddamn mouths if he starts to move again."

***

Wall found some clean cloths and put them on Suckley's face to try and stop the bleeding. Suckley was awake, but losing a lot of blood. He told him to sit tight while he went for the doctor.

He walked out the door, gun drawn and looked at Jud.

Still dead this time.

Good.

He looked at his prisoners.

"I gotta get a doctor. You boys sit tight."

Scar opened his mouth first.

"What in the hell are we gonna do if he comes back like that again? You need to free us!"

Spoon nodded.

"I just tracked your asses all over Oklahoma," Wall said. "I ain't doing it again. Besides, he's dead this time. I think."

He jumped off the porch and broke into a run.

"Well, what the hell do we do if he does come back?" Spoon yelled.

"Don't get yourself et up," Wall shouted over his shoulder.

Wall was grateful that the main part of the small Oklahoma town wasn't any bigger. He got to the doctor's office in about ten minutes running. He wished to hell he hadn't left his horse, but he wouldn't be going back to Suckley's without him.

He got the doctor-a little fat man called Doc Benson, threw him and his bag on his horse and galloped back to the undertaker's office.

"You say he *was* dead?" Doc Benson asked, trying to hold onto Wall as his horse charged through the street.

"Yes sir, deader than hell. Shot right through the heart."

"And how would you know that for sure?"

"Cos I'm the one who shot him," Wall said. "He was dead for about half an hour. He wasn't normal when he came back though."

"I've never heard of such a thing," Doc said. "I'll have to inspect the body."

"After you fix up the undertaker. He was losing a lot of blood when I left him."

"Right, right," Doc said, almost absently. "That's it there, isn't it?"

Wall nodded as they approached Suckley's office. The two men were both on the porch, looking anxious and Jud was still dead. Wall stopped the horse and tied him up, helped the doctor off of the horse and showed him up the front steps.

Doc stopped and regarded the two men.

"Why are these men chained?" he asked.

"Cos they're assholes." Wall said. "Suckley's inside."

This answer seemed to suit the Doc just fine, but not Scar and Spoon, who seemed to get angry at the remark. Wall looked at them and shrugged. He walked inside.

The rotten flower smell was now mixed with a raw coppery smell Wall figured was blood. Doc had waited for Wall to come in and lead him to Suckley. Wall walked carefully through the hall and to the little waiting room where he had left the bleeding man on a small couch.

Suckley was still there, but he wasn't moving. There was a massive pool of blood from his wound that had soaked into the peach colored couch cushion and all over the floor. The blood on the floor was mostly congealed. Benson walked past Wall and put his hand under Suckley's neck.

He felt around several times and looked back at Wall.

"This is damned strange," he said. "There's no pulse, but he's hot."

"If he's dead, shouldn't he be gettin' cold?"

"Exactly," the doctor said. "But I'd wager his temperature is over a hundred."

"That ain't natural," Wall said. Benson nodded.

As if on cue, Suckley's eyes snapped open. They had the same red and bright grey look Jud had, Wall noticed. Without thinking, Wall grabbed Benson by the arm and yanked him roughly away from Suckley, who had now begun to growl.

"Dear lord!" Doc said.

"More like Holy Shit," Wall added.

Suckley, or whatever had been Suckley, was now moving and struggling to get up. It took all he had, but Wall tamped down his instinct to leave. He passed it on to the doctor, who actually had tried to leave, but Wall held him by the arm.

"We need to leave!" Doc Benson said.

"Let's watch him a minute," Wall said. "This ain't right, but let's see what we're up against here."

Suckley kicked his feet and fell roughly onto the wooden floor. He then tried desperately to get up, which he did after a minute. He looked around the room slowly and when he saw Wall and Benson, he snarled. Wall drew his gun and pointed it at Suckley.

"Stand down, Mr. Suckley," he said. "I ain't foolin'."

Suckley lunged at the sound of his voice and Wall shot him in the heart, just like Jud. Suckley got rocked back a few steps, but he didn't fall. He started to move forward again.

Wall shot him twice more with the same result.

"Run!" Doc yelled.

"One damn minute," Wall said, calmly.

He re aimed his gun and shot Suckley between his eyes.

Suckley stood for a moment or two, but then collapsed as if all of the life was sucked out of him at once.

Nearly a full minute passed when Doc, sensing the danger had passed knelt down to Suckley and again checked his neck.

"No pulse and he's cooling off. Mr. Wall, this is very odd indeed."

Wall checked his gun barrel. He'd have to get bullets out of his saddle bag if the day kept going on this way; he took the remaining six he had in his pocket and reloaded. Holstering the gun, he looked at Suckley's body.

"I reckon, we ought to tell the law around here," Wall said.

Benson stood up and looked at Wall.

"And say what exactly?"

"That we got a problem. A big problem. I reckon that-"

Wall was interrupted by a series of knocks and kicks at the door behind him.

"What's that?" the Doc asked. Wall knew exactly what it was.

"We have to get on out of here, Doc." Wall said, grabbing Benson's arm again. "At a rapid hike."

The knocking grew louder and more intense as Wall escorted Benson out of the office.

When they reached the porch, Scar and Spoon were looking anxious. Wall drew his gun and pointed it at them.

"The doc here is gonna unshackle you boys. If either one of you tries to run, I'll part your skulls. Hear?"

They both nodded as Benson took the keys and unlocked them. The looked at each other and nodded.

"What happened to that other guy?" Spoon asked.

"Dead," Wall said and then added, "Deader now. We're going to the sheriff."

Scar scoffed.

"What the hell's she gonna do?"

"Get off the porch. You two get in front of the horse." Wall said. "And what do you mean *she*?"

When Wall was a Texas Ranger, he quickly discovered how little time was actually spent doing actual things. It had mostly been riding somewhere, arriving too late most times and then riding all the way back. He'd done it for ten years, quit and became a bounty hunter. It was nearly the same job except, in order to get paid, you had to do things. Tom loved doing things. He loved solving things and he loved coming out on top.

He also loved the idea of getting enough money to stop altogether. Maybe find a wife, have some kids and stay put for good. He'd come close a year ago to a wife and early retirement. Closer than he ever thought possible and then...

He knew he was lucky.

He also knew he missed her and was miserable about it, but there wasn't anything he could do about it.

He threw himself into his work, stopped taking rests between bounty hunts and just got on with life.

Except, it wasn't really living. It was just being alive, but it would do for now.

And as he walked quickly up the steps to see the sheriff, he thought he'd thought so hard about Veronique that he conjured her image.

Except, it was her; not just an image, but her.

She stood in a pair of dungarees that almost hid her figure and a plain shirt and vest. She wore a badge on the vest and six shooters on either side of her hips. She wore no hat, and her black hair was pulled back in a tight braid.

Wall stood there, mouth open as she looked at him. Her face was stern and he watched it soften for a moment. Then she scowled at him.

"What the hell are you doing here?" she said. Wall was dumbfounded.

"I didn't mean to be here."

"I told you not to look for me," she said.

"I wasn't. You just happened to be the sheriff in the town where I'm not looking for you."

She looked at him hard and then softened again.

"You weren't looking for me?" she asked.

Wall walked into the sheriff's office and let the door close behind him.

"Darlin', I wanted to, but I didn't even know where to start and you did say y'all would try and kill me next time. That's what we call a deterrent." She smiled and he melted.

"Listen, maybe we can talk more later, but you have a problem."

"What kind of problem?"

"Well, there ain't no way to be delicate about it. You got some dead folks running around at Suckley's." She frowned.

"What does that mean?"

"Just what I said. I shot Jud Watkins square in the chest. Dropped him on Suckley's porch with my prisoners and then, the bastard starts moving around, like he wanted to kill his two pals. Bit Suckley. Suckley wound up dying after I got the Doc. Then he came back, crazier than a shit house rat. I had to put him down."

Veronique listened calmly and nodded when Wall was done.

"You know, that sounds ridiculous." She said, finally.

It was Wall's turn to frown.

"You know me Veronique. Do I make a whole lot of jokes?"

"It's not been my experience, no." she said, trying to hide a smile. Wall smirked.

"There is some very spooky shit working its way to your town right goddamn now." He said, grabbing her arm. "You either got to get your people out, or we have to go take care of it."

He led her out into the street where the Doc and the two prisoners, now tied to the post of the Sheriff's porch, all stood looking back the way they had come.

"Mr. Wall, you ought to see this. You too Sheriff," the Doc said.

Veronique shook herself out of Wall's hand and ran to the street.

Wall stood where he was; he could guess what they saw.

"Oh no," Veronique said. "Is that what you're talking about?"

Lumbering down the street were three figures; a tall woman with what looked like a huge gash in her neck flanked by two children around ten years old with similar wounds on their arms and faces. They were slow, but they walked with purpose, looking at everything.

And snarling.

"Yeah, that's pretty much what I was talkin' about." Wall said, sadly.

"Well, don't just stand there jawin' fer Chrissakes!" Spoon said, already trying to pull himself free from the chain. "Start shootin'!"

"You can't shoot children!" Veronique said, shocked.

"They aren't children," the Doc said, never taking his eyes off of the grisly trio. "I don't know what they are, but they aren't human."

Tom nodded.

"Still, we can't just shoot 'em in the middle of the street. We have to get them off before—"

And suddenly, it was too late.

They watched in growing horror as a ten or eleven year old girl ran over to the bastardized family. The three walking corpses all turned and grabbed her before she finished saying hello.

The little girl screamed as the two boys tore at her flesh.

Wall and Veronique pulled their guns simultaneously and fired. The two flanking boys received spot on head shots as the mother, who was biting into the little girl's throat didn't react to this whatsoever.

"Nice shot," Wall said, re-aiming. He fired and the top of the mother's head flew off before she collapsed on top of the girl, who was silent and still.

The Doc stood with his mouth open as Tom ran into the street, yelling for the rest to follow him.

Spoon yelled back.

"You have to untie us you dern fool!" he said. "You're gonna get us et!" Scar spit on the ground.

"I swear, Spoon. We'd have been better off gettin' shot."

***

Wall stopped just short of the pile of bodies, gun still drawn. No one moved; everyone, including the little girl was dead. She looked up at Wall with dead, terrified eyes, blood still pouring out of her wounds. He sighed heavily and holstered his gun as Veronique stopped next to him.

"*Isis Hristos,*" Veronique whispered. "*Ceea ce monstrii sunt acestea?*"

Wall was going to ask what that meant, but he felt her grab his hand and for a moment, it didn't really matter.

"What are these things, Tom?" Veronique asked quietly.

"Ain't nothin' I ever saw." He squeezed her hand tighter and he felt her do the same. He let go and turned to the Doc, who was panting from the effort.

"We need to get these bodies out of the street," Wall said, grabbing the mother by her feet. "Things are gonna get bad enough around here. Don't need this."

The doc grabbed one of the boys and Veronique grabbed the girl. She looked at what was left of the girl and held back a cry.

She held back something else as well.

Blood streamed freely from the girl's neck as Veronique followed Tom to the back of the mercantile across the street. She felt something move inside of her and she let a small growl escape.

When she made her way to where Wall had stopped with the woman, she gently placed the little girl next to her. She stood up, shaking.

Wall looked at her.

"You know any of em?"

Veronique nodded.

"The woman is...was Millie Harper. Her boys, Stuart and Caleb. The girl..." she turned her back. "Angela Prentiss." She said through her teeth.

Wall reached out to put his hand on her shoulder, but she violently shrugged it off.

"Don't touch me," she hissed. "Not right now. I need-"

The Doc rounded the corner with the boy and his already fallen face, fell further.

"Jesus, Sheriff." He said, still dragging the boy to his mother's side. "You alright?"

Wall frowned and moved to face Veronique.

Her hands covered her face partially, but he saw enough.

Enough to jar his memory.

"Fight it," Wall whispered. "Hold it back. You can control it."

She hissed and looked at him. Her porcelain skin had grown dark, nearly black. Her grey eyes remained intact, and Wall reckoned that was a good sign.

"Pull it back, darlin'." Wall said softly. The Doc began to move closer, but Wall held out his hand.

"Stay put, Doc." He said. "Give her a minute."

The Doc frowned, but stayed.

Wall looked again at Veronique and she had begun to revert back, slowly.

"C'mon now, Sheriff." He said, smiling. "Let's see that non-sharpened smile."

All the time, Veronique stared hard at him, but at this last thing, her stare softened. Her features began to lighten and finally, she was her self— her human self—once again.

"You alright now?" Tom asked.

She responded by hugging him tightly.

"I...haven't fed in ages..." she breathed. "All of that little girl's blood...makes it hard to hold it together." Wall nodded and squeezed her.

"Can you keep it together for a little while longer?" Tom asked.

She nodded and let him go.

"I have and I will," she said. "Let's get back to the street and see if there are any more on their way."

"Now just hold on a damn minute!" the Doc said. "What in the hell was that all about?"

Wall whirled around and looked at the Doc.

"She was...changing there. She one of those...things?" The Doc asked.

"Sheriff's fine, Doc." Wall replied sternly. "Let's head out to the street and try to maintain some control here."

The look on the Doc's face was one of confusion and fear. Wall knew it was also something he wouldn't let go of either.

"But..." the Doc began, but Wall put a firm hand on his shoulder.

"But nothing." Wall said, staring at the doc. Tom's eyes were those of a dead man's-devoid of any kind of emotion. He looked deep into the Doc's eyes and spoke carefully.

"Doc, we need to concentrate on the problem at hand, not this. Sheriff's fine as you can see. What you can't see is what's going on right now and we need to get back to that right here and now. Understand?"

The doc nodded and moved to get away, but Wall's grip tightened.

"Understand me, Doc. Your sheriff is fine. The issue at hand and that's it."

The doc nodded emphatically and Wall let him go. He ran to the main street. Wall looked back at Veronique, who was walking towards him. "Let's get going, Sheriff." Wall said, waiting for her.

She smiled.

"I like how you call me Sheriff," she said.

***

"We got to bide our time, figure out when to make our move," Scar said. Spoon nodded.

"When the hell you reckon that'll be? When the rest of the goddamned dead start swarming around?" Spoon asked quietly. He didn't want anyone to hear him, even if he couldn't see anyone else around.

Scar nodded. It was a good point. Wall had kept a damn solid eye on them and even when he wasn't around, he made sure that they couldn't move anywhere. He held a chain up and threw it down in disgust.

"Next time they try and move us, we make a shot for it." Spoon agreed.

"We could take out the sheriff easy," Spoon said. "That fat ass Doc Benson doesn't look like he has much starch to him."

"Yup. Just gotta worry about Wall," Scar said. He thought he might have an idea, but Doc Benson, Veronique and Wall had walked back into view.

"You boys behaving?" Wall yelled.

The two men said nothing.

"Figured," Wall said, looking at Veronique. "You reckon we can shove these assholes in your jail for a bit?" Veronique nodded.

"Plenty of room," she said and walked towards the two men.

Scar nodded slightly to Spoon who tried to hide a smile.

"So you don't think you're clever," Veronique said as she approached the two men. "If you try anything, I'll kill you where you stand. And then, I'll eat you."

Wall didn't bother hiding a smile.

Scar scoffed.

"Just what the hell do you think you can-"

As Scar was speaking, Spoon made his move. He had grabbed his chain and tried to loop it around Veronique's neck.

Except, she wasn't there when he went to grab her.

The next thing that happened was Spoon was kneeling in the dirt, grabbing his throat as was Scar. Veronique stood quietly three feet away. The Doc rubbed his eyes as Tom looked on in mild amazement.

"I wasn't kidding, gentlemen." She said. "Now get up, or I'll hit you hard next time."

Wall chuckled and walked over.

"I think they get the point, right boys?"

The two coughed painfully and stood up.

"Hell," Wall said. "Her jail might be the safest place for you two. I wouldn't try nothin' else."

Scar nodded but Spoon just glared.

After moving the men into the jail, Wall, Veronique and Doc sat around Veronique's desk to discuss options.

"Ain't a whole lot of options here, folks." Doc said.

Wall shook his head.

"There's got to be some reason for this, and we find that, we get a lead on how to stop it before it gets worse."

Veronique looked out of her window to the street. It was empty.

"I ain't never heard of nothing like this," Wall said.

"I have." Veronique said quietly.

Doc coughed and sat up straight.

"I beg pardon?" he asked.

"What are you talking about?" Wall asked.

Veronique didn't look at the men, but began to speak.

"I was born in Slovenia, then grew up in Romania, but when I was still a little girl my father moved us to Moldavia for better work. In Moldavia, there was a legend of a thing called the strigoi. It was where the vampire legend originated, although we know those aren't real...don't we?"

Tom put his head down for a moment and let her continue.

"The original legend was that a strigoi was both human and demon. Dead yet alive. These things could be *strigoi mort*, but not exactly."

"Okay, so why would they suddenly just show up here in the middle of goddamn nowhere?" Doc asked. "You seem to know about them, but who else would?"

Veronique took a deep breath.

"Bosen," Wall said. "He from your village?"

Veronique shook her head.

"He wasn't, but Bosen makes sense," Veronique said. "He was furious after I burned the town down. We parted company after that and I did my best to vanish." Veronique said.

"You think he found you?" Wall asked.

"Again, it would make sense. He swore he'd kill me if he ever found me."

The Doc coughed and slammed a fist down on the desk.

"You want to include me in this goddamn conversation please?" Doc said, angrily.

Tom cleared his throat.

"This fella Bosen we know might be responsible for this. We find him, we got a shot of stopping what's going on."

"But, what's this about burning down a town?"

"It don't matter," Wall said. "We need to concentrate on right now, not back then."

Veronique sat up straight, still looking out the window.

"Meeting's over," she said. "We have more coming into town."

Both men looked out of the window and saw seven folks walking in the distance. Five men, one woman and a boy; all dead and walking down the street.

Wall sighed and pulled his gun to check how many rounds he had left.

Four in the chamber, and a box on his horse.

Veronique seemed to have read his mind. She walked to the gun cabinet behind the desk and unlocked it. She pulled out a double barrel shot gun and a second colt, which she tucked into her pants.

"Take what you need," she said to Wall. She regarded the Doc and said, "Take what you think you can handle."

"Just ammo," he said getting out of his chair.

"But how do you know this Bosen person? What kind of man can-" Wall shushed him.

"Later, Doc. Trust me. You don't want to be in any kind of rush to find out what kind of man he is,"

This made Doc swallow hard. He stood up and grabbed a handgun.

"Everything here is a nightmare," the Doc said to himself.

Wall, Veronique and the Doc walked into the center of the street to meet the seven dead folks shambling in their direction.

"I don't think they see us," Wall said.

"How the hell do *you* know?" Doc said a lot louder than he intended.

At the sound of his voice, all seven heads snapped to their general direction. They snarled in unison and began to shamble with purpose.

"Call it a goddamn hunch," Wall said, disgusted. He pulled his gun which was now loaded. "I'll meet them up there. You two hang back here in case there are any surprises." He looked at Veronique, who stood her ground but nodded.

Wall smiled.

"Is that alright, Sheriff? I know I'm a little out of my jurisdiction,"

Veronique smiled back.

"As it says in your adventures, your jurisdiction is wherever you happen to be."

She winked.

Wall turned and walked toward the seven ghouls, gun drawn and trying to calm himself down. His mind was racing with what was in front of him but also of what was behind him.

The five men shambled behind the two children. They were all covered in dried blood and gunshot wounds. The girl's jaw hung slack as if someone had tried to wrench it off and finally, gave up.

The wind blew gently down the street and with it, a stench that hit Wall like a shovel to the face. He stopped for a moment, fought a gag and steeled himself to move forward.

He walked slowly, trying to decide which of them to shoot first; he had the luxury of time as they shambled down the road, but then he noticed that each one of them had something around their necks.

Signs.

He could make the signs out the closer he got, but they must have gotten out of order.

TO THE
THE WHORE
EATEN
STABLES
BRING
BE OR

It didn't take long to translate it, but by the time he did, they were almost on him. He drew his gun about fifteen feet out and fired.

Click.

"Aw hell," Wall said as the boy snarled at him.

"What in the hell is he waiting for?" Doc asked, watching the scene unfold.

Veronique cocked the shotgun and began to run to Wall, who was checking his gun and backing up.

"Sheriff, don't!" yelled Doc, who didn't have to fight hard to stay where he stood. "He said to wait here!"

She didn't answer and ran faster.

Much faster than Doc would have thought possible.

She slowed down about ten feet behind Wall just as he holstered his gun and drew a knife.

The boy, who moved faster than the other six, lunged for Wall as he pulled his arm back and stabbed the little boy in the side of his skull.

The boy made a small grunting sound and fell, sliding off of the knife, black goo spilling from the wound.

Wall gagged, but didn't retch. Still he rested his hand on his knee as the other six approached, all snarling.

The shotgun exploded behind him and he whirled around to see Veronique, gun poised. She motioned for him to turn back around.

He did and saw one of the men missing a large portion of his head. The thing dropped to its knees and fell over forward.

Down to five.

"Don't fire," Wall said as he launched himself at the nearest thing, stabbing it in the head with the knife.

Wall quickly dispatched the rest of the ghouls and sat down in the road. Veronique came up behind him and put a hand on his head.

They were silent for a moment until Wall said, "Did you read the signs?"

"I saw they had them, but didn't read. I wanted to stop them from attacking you."

"Well," he said. "It was a message. Words were all jumbled, but it said 'Bring the whore to the stables or be eaten.'"

Veronique stood quietly.

"Bosen," she said.

"Be damned surprised if it weren't."

She took her hand off of his head.

"I guess I shall go to the stables then," she said. "I have to protect my town."

Wall got up from the ground and stood in front of her.

"You ain't going alone."

"Yes Tom, I am. It's me he wants."

"He's gotta go through me first."

She smiled weakly.

"You're sweet, but no. This is my fight."

"Our fight." He corrected.

She grabbed him and kissed him deeply. When she pulled back, she was crying.

"You were a dream, Tom."

"You're still mine, and I ain't no dream. I'm right here."

She stroked his face.

"Monsters don't get to have dreams."

"I don't see no monster in front of me."

"But there is one in front of you. That's just it. That's why you're a dream for me. A dream I won't ever get to have."

Tom cleared his throat.

"I got dreams. Dreams with you in them. We don't have to go to those stables at all. We can just go."

"Dreams don't come true," she said looking away.

"Didn't your Momma ever tell you to believe in your dreams?" Veronique laughed a bitter laugh.

"Yes, yes she did. Until we moved to Moldavia. But I believed in them. All the time. Then I became...this," She held out her arms. "A monster in girl's dressings. I dreamed about being normal again all the time. I thought I just didn't believe in my dreams enough. Then I thought that I wasn't trying hard enough to live up to my dreams. But now? Now I'm thinking that sometimes your dreams have a hard time believing in you. Maybe you don't abandon your dreams as much as they abandon you and that just...broke my heart. So, no. My dreams are dreams, nothing more."

Tom stared at her sadly. Then he grabbed her and kissed her. He pulled back smiling at her.

"Alright. No dreams. This is real life then, and I want you in mine. Monster? I don't know that. I know your heart. Whatever the hell else you are doesn't matter much to me."

She smiled.

"By the way," he said. "Your name. You crossed it off on your letter. Viorica?"

"It was, when I was a little girl." she said. "Not anymore."

"I'll call you whatever you want," He said. "It'll probably wind up bein' darlin' anyway."

"You aren't coming with me to the stables," she said.

"Damn right," he said and punched her as hard as he could in the jaw.

She fell backwards, knocked out cold.

He picked her up and walked down and met up with Doc.

"Thanks for all your help, Doc," Wall said as Doc stared blankly at him. "Open up that goddamn door. She ain't as light as she looks."

Doc didn't bother to protest and opened the door. Wall brought her in and lay her on the floor behind her desk. He stood back up, grabbed a shotgun, some shells and faced Doc.

"You listen here. I'm going to end this thing. You are not to let her out of this building, you hear me? No matter what she tells you, you keep her here."

"What about us?" Spoon yelled from the jail.

Wall ignored him.

"Why'd you hit her?" Doc asked.

"Cos she can't go where I'm going. Under any circumstances. Only way to do it."

"Well, she's a girl. She ought to just listen."

Wall smiled.

"Yeah, not this one. Try to keep her here."

He walked out of the door and said on his way out,

"But whatever you do, don't piss her off."

***

Wall neared the stables on the other end of the town, and heard the horses neighing restlessly.

No, not neighing...*screaming*.

He forced himself to not break into a run, but the louder the screams became, the harder it was to resist.

Resist he did, but someone else didn't need to resist.

"What in tarnation is that?" said an older man of about 49 running past Wall.

So much for not being seen, Wall thought.

He watched the man round the corner of the stable and then heard him, scream briefly and then was silent Even the sound of the horses was lessening now. Thick, black smoke and a sickly sweet smell began to hit Wall's nose and he knew what it was; roasting meat.

He swallowed hard and crept up to the back of the stable and worked his way around to catch a glimpse of what was happening.

Wall's eyes began to burn from the smoke, but it didn't stop the visual he was seeing. He doubted he'd ever be able to *unsee* it.

In the center of the horses pen were four things; something that looked like a large metal bridge, horses, dead folks and a huge fire underneath the bridge.

The horses were being driven onto the bridge and over the fire where they were being roasted alive. Wall could see that some of the dead folk had caught on fire as well just from stumbling into it. But, the dead folk were also eating the horses that weren't on the bridge and it was taking a long time. The pen had been reinforced, the horses couldn't get away. Several horses were strewn along the fence line either dead or dying. The coppery smell of blood and smoke choked the air around him. There didn't seem to be any purpose for this atrocity and that alone made Wall furious. He fought nausea hard and scanned the area for Bosen.

He saw no one that wasn't already dead, but he did see the man who had run ahead of him lying on his back, dead.

Then, he twitched and began to move.

Wall couldn't look anymore and turned away to walk back behind the stable to figure out what to do.

He walked two steps and saw him.

It wasn't Bosen.

"Hello Tom," Hank the bartender said.

Tom raised the shotgun, but Hank reached out lightning fast and pulled it out of his hands. Hank threw the shotgun far and away behind him. "You ought to know better than that," Hank said, not smiling. "Yeah, well I guess I don't learn very well. Maybe next time." This time, Hank did smile.

"Ain't gonna be no next time, bounty hunter," Hank said. "Where's the whore?"

"Where's Bosen?" Wall asked.

"Bosen? Hell, he's dead," Hank said, laughing a little. "Took care of him after I tracked down the whore. Said he wanted to leave her be, after seeing what she was doing here." Wall blinked.

"Doing what?"

"You remember when I last saw you? Bosen gave you all that bullshit about what we were trying to do?"

Wall nodded so Hank continued.

"How he loved this country and wanted to give back by only killin' the criminals? He convinced most of us that was the way to go, stay out of the light. Well, after everything I've been through, I say to hell with that. How do you stay quiet and hid when you used to be feared like a god?"

"So you killed him. What happened to the rest of them?"

"I killed *all* of them," Hank said and gave Wall a cold look. "Every last damn one of them. They want to live like a secret, then they can buried like a damn secret too. Just one last loose end to tie."

Wall nodded and swallowed.

"Well, I guess two loose ends. You'll be the easiest one."

"The horses. Why did you do that?"

Hank smiled a sick smile.

"Know what a *strigoi* is, Wall?"

"Sort of," he said.

"No shit, really?" Hank was genuinely surprised. "Looks like you're more educated than I thought you were. Me? I'm a strigoi, but these are *strigoi mort*. That's these dead fellers. Now tell me, you know how to make one? Or a dozen? It's a lot more simple than you'd think."

"I reckon burning horses is a part of it," Wall said, disgusted.

"Close. It's committing an obscene act in front of the eyes of God. So obscene, that the very *after effect* of it causes the dead to rise out of *protest*. That's what I've done here. Frankly, I'm glad you showed up cos I was running out of horses."

"In case you were wonderin'," Wall said looking Hank right in the eyes. "I'm gonna have to put you down for this."

The look was such that Hank stepped back. Wall's eyes were cold, dead and terrifying. After a moment, Hank broke into a smile.

"I seem to have you at a disadvantage, Wall. I took your gun and I'm damn sure gonna eat the hell out of you here shortly. A spooky set of eyes ain't gonna do shit."

Wall smiled. It was nearly as cold as his eyes.

"You ain't gotta worry about my eyes if that's where you're looking," Wall said and quickly reached around to the back holster he'd made a few years ago. His arm swung back around with a two shot Derringer and popped a bullet into Hank's knee.

Hank howled in agony as he dropped to the ground clutching his knee. Wall moved in closer and kicked Hank as hard as he could in the face.

Twice.

Hank bled out of his knee slowly as he lay unconscious.

Wall grabbed him by the hands and started to drag him to the other side of the stable.

His plan was to drag Hank over by the pen and hope some of the dead folk would gnaw on him for a little bit while Wall figured out how to save the rest of the horses. Then he could worry about taking care of the rest of the dead folk.

Wall got halfway to the pen when Hank suddenly came back to the land of the awake. His hands twisted and grabbed Wall's wrists tightly. Wall was then yanked forward and thrown about thirty feet. He landed next to the burning corral.

He rolled and felt his ribs shift in his chest. He hissed in pain, but got to his feet as fast as he could and saw Hank start to change.

"Guess you ain't that smart after all," Hank said in a deepening voice. His skin started to crack and peel as the transformation began.

Wall had only seen the earliest part of the transformation when Veronique was changing; he had only seen part of her face mid-transformation before the darkness took him and he saw no more until he woke up hours later.

This time, he was watching the whole thing.

And it was horrifying.

Hank's face turned into a rictus of fangs and his skin cracked and fell off, exposing a black hard looking exterior. His arms unhinged and nearly detached as they extended. He looked very much like a spider with four legs instead of eight. Hank's clothes ripped and fell off as the transformation went on; it lasted no more than 15 seconds, but it felt like an eternity to Wall.

The nearly ten foot tall Hank-thing reared back and screamed.

Wall nearly screamed too, but he was looking for something-anything to use to fight it off.

The thing screamed at him again.

"Shut your goddamned trap and just get on with it!" Wall yelled. "Go on and try to eat me, but give my ears a rest you ugly son of a bitch!"

Another scream bellowed out, but this time it wasn't from the Hank thing. It came from further away. As the Hank thing turned, Wall immediately knew what it was.

Veronique.

Transformed.

And Wall smiled.

The Veronique-thing was bigger than the Hank-thing and the Hank-thing shuddered visibly as she quickly filled the space between the two.

Something like a whine came out of the Hank-thing as it was lifted up by the other creature. The Veronique-thing began to twist the Hank-thing until it simply ripped in half. The Hank-thing screamed as its insides poured out onto the ground. Where it hit the ground, it sizzled as if it were some sort of acid.

The Veronique-thing screamed something that sounded like a word, but Wall couldn't make it out. Suddenly, in the center of Wall's head he heard Veronique's voice loudly and clearly.

Move!

Grunting in pain, he staggered away from the burning corral and Veronique threw what was left of Hank into the fire. The fire exploded as if someone had dumped gallons of whisky on it. Everything in the corral was incinerated and the force of the blast knocked Wall to the ground. His world went black.

***

Wall opened his eyes slowly to a half obscured blue sky and black smoke. There was a figure standing over him and he could see who it was.

He coughed. His ribs and back sang out in agony and he rolled over to cough harder. He hadn't hurt this bad in his memory. He saw two naked legs that he hoped to hell were Veronique's.

"Are you okay?" she said.

Wall tried not to laugh so he threw up instead. He saw that she was backing up.

He turned his head and looked up. She was naked, getting dressed.

"Good morning," he croaked and she laughed.

"Are you okay?" she asked again.

"Hell *no* I ain't okay," he said and struggled to stand. "Gotta get them horses out of that damn thing,"

"I took care of the horses," she said and helped him up.

He leaned on her and she pointed him to the stable bard, where eight nervous looking, but alive horses stood together looking around, wondering possibly why they were still alive.

"Thanks," Wall said and looked at her.

She smiled at him. She looked better than when he had first laid eyes on her that day.

"You look better," he said. "Not just because you're naked."

She put her head down and said, "I have bad news about your two prisoners."

"They somehow met a fate worse than a hanging?"

"I needed to save you," she said. "I haven't fed since the last time I saw you. We can live without feeding like that, but...we aren't as strong. I couldn't take Bosen without being strong...or Hank as it turns out"

He looked at her and then turned to look at the corral. It was still burning, but it was finally dying down.

There were corpses, but thankfully no longer moving.

He looked at Veronique.

"Finally saw you," he said.

She looked up at him.

"And?"

He smiled.

"Least I didn't pass out this time," he said.

"I'm a monster," She said.

"You saved my life,"

"I'm a *monster*," she repeated.

"No," Wall said, putting his hand on her face. "Hank was a monster. He was killing folks to try and kill you. You were trying to do good in spite of what you think. He was raising the dead, slaughtering horses and such. He's the monster. You didn't ask to be what you are." She smiled weakly.

"I was turned into this, and there isn't a way to turn back."

"Well, we'll figure out how to live with it I reckon." He said and kissed her forehead. "It might come in handy."

"What do you mean, 'we?'"

He guided her away from the wreckage and began to walk away from it.

"I ain't letting you slink off this time, woman." He said through his teeth. "This seems like a halfway decent town to live...well, now that all the dead folks are dead."

"Well, I don't know Captain Wall," she said. "I might have a small issue with you hitting me a while back there,"

He coughed.

"Yeah, sorry about that. I couldn't think of what else to do."

She stopped and pulled his face to hers. She kissed him long and deep, then pulled back.

"I think I know something else we can do,"

He smiled.

"I don't know how that's gonna work with my ribs, darlin' " he said. "That's gonna hurt I think."

She smiled.

"Well, I didn't eat the Doc. He's back at his office where I sent him to wait for us. He'll take a look at you. And *then* we'll see how bad it's gonna hurt."

They walked away, holding each other and very decidedly not looking back at what they had already seen. They were looking forward to something new for the first time in a long time.

CHAPTER 5

Corpus Christi, Texas 1885

Wall stood, looking at the new home Veronique and he had built. They'd been there roughly a month and he couldn't recall ever being happier. Veronique was still inside, sleeping. The slow lazy Texas sun was rising up over the ocean he couldn't see, but sure could smell. On quiet nights, he could hear it and that was just about the best thing he'd ever heard with the exception of his love sleeping next to him.

He looked at the house and the big tree on the right of it. It was a gnarled looking tree with red leaves and berries. He had been hesitant of putting the house right next to the on account of the birds eating the berries. There was a similar tree next to the shack where he grew up. The birds would eat the berries and then shit red all over the place. Veronique had requested that the tree stay where it was as she thought it was beautiful.

"Can you make jelly from them berries?" he asked.

"Well, I think I can," she said smiling. "But I think they'd taste awful."

"Give it a try anyway," he said. "I do like me some jelly."

She had done as he asked, but she had been right. The jelly was awful and although it was, Veronique had made twenty some jars of it. He forced himself to eat through one jar, but couldn't abide the others. He put them out into the barn so he didn't accidentally eat some of it. Also, Veronique had some kind of awful allergic reaction to it. She was sick as a dog for about a week after she'd made it. Since they really couldn't take her to a doctor or anything, she stayed in bed and Tom brought her things she needed, including some small live game.

When she got better, she'd also spend a lot of time tending to flowers in their new place. Mostly, daffodils. She loved those flowers something awful and even though Wall didn't particularly like the color yellow, they sure looked good when they'd started coming in bloom.

This was a life he'd never thought possible from his days as a Texas Ranger or a bounty hunter. No looking over his shoulder, no more sleeping on the goddamn ground. No one looking for him and him not looking for anyone. He was happily retired. He had a wife, a house and a goddamn tree that made *awful* goddamn jelly. He was happy for the very first time.

As the sun rose higher, he slowly walked towards the house. As his eyes wandered around, he saw a figure in the doorway. It was Veronique.

She was gloriously naked.

"Have I told you how much I love living so far away from other people?" she called out to him.

Wall smiled.

"Why, Mrs. Wall," he said. "You don't have a stitch of clothing on you."

He was smiling.

"Well, the only one who can see me is you." She said.

"I'm pretty happy about that," he said.

"Not as happy as you're going to be once you get in the house." She said and disappeared from view.

"I reckon that's true," he said to himself as he walked quickly to the porch.

Things were finally good.

Safe.

Home.

PART TWO:
SPIDERS IN THE DAFFODILS

"Deep in each man is the knowledge that something knows of his existence. Something knows, and cannot be fled nor hid from."

— Cormac McCarthy

CHAPTER 1

Odessa, Texas 1895

Stephan Trask didn't mean to throw the sheriff through the front of the saloon window. It just happened to work out that way.

Trask fancied himself a peaceful man, but it was hard to argue that point with the patrons of the Goshen Saloon who had just witnessed such a thing.

Sheriff Bowler had simply asked Trask to kindly pay his tab and exit the saloon. Something Trask would have normally been willing to do without issue. To be fair, Trask had been tired; he'd been playing poker for about ten hours straight after arriving from Galveston the day previous. And, he'd been winning.

A lot.

The players all had begun to suspect that their new poker "friend" had been cheating. All of them cheated of course. It would have been almost rude to not cheat, but the manner in which Trask had been cheating was a complete mystery to all involved.

That was unacceptable, unless he was willing to share.

And Trask was *not* inclined to share.

So the sheriff had been sent for when Trask's lack of sharing had been questioned.

It should have gone a lot quieter.

Trask sat with his back to the saloon door, smoking a cigar and drinking cheap whisky waiting for the next hand of cards to start. He had heard the sheriff enter and walk to the bar to talk to the bartender.

Judging by the fall of the sheriff's footsteps, Trask reckoned the man was at least over two hundred pounds and a little over six feet tall. From the sheriff's breathing, he also figured he was nearly in his forties and grossly out of shape.

Words were exchanged and Trask pretended to ignore it, but he heard every word of it and smirked.

He decided that he wouldn't make a scene. He would grab his things and his money and quietly leave with the sheriff. It was the plan. Besides, it wasn't worth getting into a fight with a man so very much incapable.

"You Steven Trask?" the sheriff said behind him.

"It's *Stephan*, and yes. I'm Trask."

The sheriff took a moment to spit on the floor casually.

"Name's Sheriff Bowler, Mr. Trask. Need to talk to you in my office," he said. "We don't want no trouble here, so if you'd pay your tab and come along all peaceful like, I'd surely appreciate it."

Trask was about to tell Bowler he would come along quietly and that there would be no issue at all.

Then, Sheriff Bowler put his hand on Trask's shoulder.

What happened next occurred so fast, Bowler didn't know something had actually happened until he was going through the window.

The hand sat on his shoulder for half a second as Trask inhaled from his cigar. Trask grabbed the sheriff's hand while rising from his chair. As he rose, he bent the sheriff's wrist back almost to his arm, snapping the bone and opening the skin. Trask, who still had not fully risen, then spun and grabbed Bowler by his collar bone tightly. He lifted the man off of his feet, breaking the collarbone. He whipped completely around and flung Bowler through the plate glass window of the saloon, which was a good ten feet away. Very few people actually saw it, which was temporarily in Trask's favor.

As the very last piece of glass hit the hardwood floor, Trask took the cigar out of his mouth and exhaled.

"Well, damn." Trask said. He didn't have to look around the room to know all eyes were on him. He regarded the shocked poker table and smiled. "I guess our friendly game has come to a sudden conclusion, gentlemen."

He carefully picked up his money and walked to the bar. He put down a wad of cash down on the counter and looked coolly at the bartender.

"For the damages, plus the drinks. Also, buy these folks a round on me. Oh, and one more thing,"

He took an additional pile of cash from his winnings and stuffed into the bartender's shirt pocket.

"For the sheriff and his injuries," Trask said. "No hard feelings."

He smiled and turned to face the patrons.

"Guess I'll be on my way," Trask said loudly. "Had a lovely time, folks."

He turned towards the saloon doors when the deputy walked in, gun drawn.

"You just wait a goddamned *minute*," the deputy said. He was a younger man and from the looks, quite inexperienced. It was easy to spot. A very thin smile broke out onto Trask's face.

"Why, deputy. I was hoping to have cleared out by the time you got here."

"Put your hands on the bar," the deputy said, visibly shaking.

"Now, there's no need for this, young man. It's quite a misunderstanding."

The deputy did a double take.

"Misunderstanding, my *ass!*" the deputy said. "Mister, I don't know what the hell you and your friends did to the sheriff, but he's damn near dead out there. The doc's on his way, so you and whoever else threw that man out of the window line up along that bar. Now."

The bartender walked over to the far part of the bar.

"Clyde," he said. "It was him. Ain't no one else *but him.*"

The Deputy looked at the bartender. Then he looked back at Trask.

Trask wasn't a tall man and had an average build. But, he looked frightening if you looked at him too long. Short blonde, nearly white hair, pale skin and bright blue eyes. The Deputy watched as this man smiled and it sent a shiver through him.

"Ain't no way, Bill. Sheriff's damn near in the middle of the street."

Trask moved forward, starting to smile a little broader.

"No, the barkeep is quite correct, deputy." Trask said. "And believe it or not, I didn't mean any harm. I sure hope he recovers and I really think you need to back off now, son."

The deputy pulled the hammer back on the gun.

"Put your goddamn hands on the bar, son." The deputy said, gritting his teeth.

"You saw what I did to your sheriff," Trask said. "And that was a pure accident. What do you think I'm going to do to *you?*"

The deputy, having Trask dead to rights, fired his gun.

He blinked and Trask was gone.

Not dead, but physically gone from sight.

The Deputy looked around the saloon and saw open mouths, staring in disbelief at him.

"You couldn't help yourself, deputy." Trask said, suddenly standing right next to him. He grabbed the gun and tore it out of the deputy's hand. "I can understand that,"

Before he could react, Trask grabbed the side of the deputy's head with one hand and with the other, drove the gun, barrel first into his temple. The Deputy didn't have time to even scream as he felt the barrel break through his skull. It made a sound like someone shoving a broomstick handle into a watermelon. The deputy shook uncontrollably, wavered and then collapsed onto the floor. His eyes were wide open and a thin line of drool fell into a growing pool that also was filling with blood.

Trask looked up and regarded the saloon again, this time not smiling.

"You folks don't have any other lawmen lining up in this town do you?" Trask asked.

No one said a word.

"Well," Trask said. "I reckon that says it all."

He turned to walk out of the saloon, but turned back around

"Oh, I'm taking somebody's horse. Not stealing it. If you want it back, I'll leave it for you in Corpus Christi," He said. "Wait about three weeks though. And don't come looking for it too soon."

He nodded and walked out of the saloon.

The patrons, the poker players, the barkeep and even the whores in the upper rooms all held their breath and looked at the Deputy, spilling blood all over the saloon floor.

No one dared to breathe.

CHAPTER 2

Corpus Christi, Texas

Tom Wall crouched behind a barn door left slightly ajar. For all intents and purposes, he was pinned down. No gun, no help for miles. He'd been in more situations like this than he'd ever expected, but this one seemed more important.

He could tell because this time, he was smiling.

Smiling was something the former Texas Ranger did very little of during his career. He was arguably one of the best Rangers that had ever lived and when he quit while he was still relatively young-a rare thing indeed for his line of work, he became better known as a bounty hunter.

He was neither of these things anymore, but the instinct was still there. The unused parts of his being that had kept him alive eagerly sprang forward and came to life.

He hadn't felt this good in a long time.

He heard footsteps slowly shuffle toward the barn and his body coiled. He was ready for anything.

"You best come out of there," he heard a voice. "Don't want no trouble."

Wall's smile grew.

"You're out of your jurisdiction," Wall called out.

He heard a quick shuffling of feet then a deathly cold silence. He strained his ear but there was a sudden silence as if everything that could move, including the wind, stopped.

He felt something hard press into his back.

"My jurisdiction is wherever I happen to be," the voice said, giggling.

Wall turned to the nine year old girl, holding a stick like a pistol. She had his mouth and her mother's eyes and apparently, a lot of her stealth.

"I got you Daddy!" she squealed. Wall laughed and grabbed her. He pulled her into his arms and hugged her tightly.

"By God, you did, darlin'," he said. "You're getting really good, you know that?"

She dropped the stick and hugged him back.

"You really think so?"

"Well, of course I do. You could make quite a Ranger when you're older."

A smirk crossed his daughter Josephine's face.

"Momma said they don't let girls be Rangers,"

"Your Momma used to be sheriff of a whole town you know." Wall said, picking up the girl and standing. "Ain't nobody told her she couldn't be sheriff. I reckon by the time you're old enough, you can be anything you want."

He began to walk out of the barn and toward the house. Josephine began to play with her father's hair and he chuckled.

"Quit that," he said. "Your Momma is the only one allowed to do that,"

"And me!" she said. He took her and began to toss her around, upside down and sideways as she giggled uncontrollably. They played like this often and it was part of why Tom Wall was a much different man than he'd ever thought he'd be.

So much of his life had been surrounded by poverty and violence, even before joining the Texas Rangers. The Rangers saved him from the poverty he grew up in, but it introduced him to a level of violence he'd never thought possible. Violence he'd always wanted to be free of and never could until now.

And he wasn't going to let it get away from him.

Not this time.

As they approached the house, Veronique stood in the doorway, smiling as she watched her husband and child laughing up a storm.

Back then they were always saving one another somehow. It was an exciting time, but dangerous too. His life as a bounty hunter had seen him leave for weeks, sometimes months at a time and her job as a Sheriff didn't make things any easier.

Of course, there was also the fact of what she was....*still* was and always would be.

"She got me again," Wall said as he climbed the porch, dangling Josephine by her two feet as she screamed with delight.

"Of course she did," Veronique said. "It's in her blood, is it not?"

"Daddy, put me down," Josephine said.

He lowered the little girl a bit and then suddenly threw her into the air, catching her under her arms and setting her down gently on the porch.

She ran to Veronique, hugging her at the waist.

"Go clean up, *floare.*" She said to Josephine, and the little girl ran through the house to the washing basin.

"Me too?" Wall asked, walking closer to his wife.

"Maybe later," she said. "We can clean each other a bit later perhaps after our little one is asleep."

Wall smiled and kissed Veronique deeply.

"That sounds like a good idea, darlin'." He said.

She giggled and slid her arms around him.

"You always think that's a good idea,"

"Ain't been wrong yet," he said.

"True, love." she said, kissing him back.

Wall pulled back after a time and looked into his wife's eyes.

"She's starting to show some more signs," he said.

A dour look crossed her face.

"This doesn't bother you?"

Wall chuckled.

"Well, maybe a little but not for the reasons you might think."

"Explain," she said, a little harder than she wanted.

"Well," Wall began. "She's fast. *Damn* fast. She cleared the distance of about fifteen feet and snuck up on me from behind without me seeing or hearing her. Sound familiar?"

Veronique opened her mouth to say that it did, but stopped herself.

"I think this is just the tip of the iceberg, darlin'." Wall said. "She is her Momma's daughter."

"And she's her Father's daughter too." Veronique replied sharply. "She's stubborn and reckless."

"Don't get all mad, we knew this was a possibility. And we said we'd deal with it when it came up. Well, it's come up." Wall said.

Veronique pulled away from him.

"You don't know what it's like, Tom. I never wanted this for her."

"Well, I ain't exactly jumpin' up and down about it either, but we knew it could happen."

Veronique allowed a single tear escape her eye.

"I don't want my baby to be...a..." She couldn't finish.

Wall reached out and grabbed her, pulling her close and hugging her.

"Shhhh," he said, trying to soothe her. "She ain't no monster and neither are you."

She pulled away from him.

"How do you love me, knowing what I am?" she asked.

"I love you," he began. "With everything I have left in me. And that's a lot more than I ever thought I ever had. You saved me."

She looked at him, sadly.

"I nearly got you killed."

"You wouldn't have killed me, and that's not what I'm talking about. You know what I mean."

She nodded.

"You just don't understand, Tom."

"I'm a lot better at understanding it than you give me credit for sometimes."

She stared at him.

"You are infuriating sometimes," she said.

"Well, likewise." He said smiling. "But you can get mad at me all you want, don't make me wrong. We've been through a lot, darlin'. We fought to get here and we won."

"But what about Josephine? Shouldn't she get a chance to win?"

"Who says she don't get to win?" Wall asked. "Far as I'm concerned, that's her call. We teach her how to control whatever she gets from you. I ain't gonna worry about it, Veronique. She's got both of us to keep an eye on her. More than I ever had,"

"But, she'll be alone," she said. "I grew up a monster and I didn't have anything or anyone. Just misery."

Wall smiled.

"Until you met me. I was the same way. I reckon, she has a much better shot than either one of us did."

She looked at him hard.

"How the hell can you be so optimistic?" she asked.

Wall smiled.

"Because my wife likes me that way. So does my daughter. How's that for an answer?"

"You married a monster," she said.

"So did you," Wall replied.

"What's a monster?" Josephine said, suddenly from behind them.

Wall smiled.

"Not you or your Momma," he said, picking up Veronique and twirling her. With that, she couldn't help but to giggle. No one had ever picked her up, much less twirled her around the way Wall did, and he did this often to mostly her delight.

This was one of those times.

Wall was the first man she had ever trusted and there had never been a reason to doubt him before. She certainly wasn't going to start now, but the very fact of what she was and what her daughter was turning into made her worry.

She'd spent the past ten years trying to explain to him what she could about what it was that made her different. For the most part, she had only scratched the surface of it mainly because she wasn't too sure herself.

But, now wasn't the time to worry; things were good. She'd managed to contain what was inside her and someday, she'd have to teach Josephine to do the same. She hoped she wouldn't have to, but after what Wall had told her, she'd have to figure that out sooner than expected.

It was something Wall wouldn't be able to help with, that she knew as well and it made her sad.

As Wall continued to twirl her and as she watched her young beautiful daughter laughing, her sadness was relieved for a moment.

It would come up again, of course. There was no stopping that she knew, but for the moment, all in the world was right.

This would have to do for the time being, and it made her smile.

She wasn't in a rush to have her little girl grow up too fast, or anytime soon. Or, for that matter, have her husband stop spinning her around.

***

Later that evening, Veronique and Josephine cleaned the table after dinner as Wall sat on the front porch, drinking coffee and starting out across the horizon. It was early June and the evening was clear. The sounds of the ocean gently floated in the air and Wall smiled.

Wall had been known as cold, hard man. He was tall, lean and muscular, but not large. He was intimidating to be sure, but what made him feared were his eyes. But now, his eyes were softer and laugh lines had begun to form. He was a changed man and he had been the happiest he'd ever been for the last ten years.

He breathed in the lightly salted air and closed his eyes. The feeling of peace he felt was almost unnerving. It couldn't be real. He knew it was, but the world wasn't made to be like this and the fear he held at bay was that something would come along and prove him right.

The thought of this sent a chill through him. He wanted nothing more than to just vanish into the new life he and Veronique had made for themselves. But, he also knew that something would come and drag them back into the life they had both desperately tried to escape.

It was just a matter of when.

He heard the porch door open and from the footsteps he heard, he knew instantly who it was.

"Hi, little darlin'," he said, smiling again.

"Hi Daddy." She said and walked over to him, crawling into his lap.

"What are you doing?" Josephine asked.

"Ain't doin' a whole lot of anything." He said. "Just enjoying the evening."

She looked up at him and frowned.

"Were you crying Daddy?"

Wall chuckled.

"I don't know. My face wet or something?"

"No," she said. "You just look really sad."

Wall hugged her tightly.

"How am I gonna be sad when I live with two of the prettiest girls in Texas?"

***

Veronique lay on Wall's chest, listening to him breathe. It remained one of her favorite things to do. When they had made love for the first time, years ago, she had done the same thing and fell in love with this odd, beautiful man.

It was a very dark time in her life and when she had met him, she thought she would have to kill him. She wouldn't have given it a single thought, killing him. She'd done it before without flinching.

Veronique looked at her man and sighed.

She'd been through so much and probably wouldn't have made it through without knowing this man. She had never had hope of such happiness especially with who she was...and what she was.

A monster.

Wall had begun to stir in his sleep. She kissed his chest and began to stoke his face. He calmed, and began to snore again. It had become her favorite sound, next to Josephine's little girl snores.

She looked at him. He wouldn't change. Not his heart, nor his appearance. He'd get older, sure. But he wouldn't be a monster. Even if his mood grew ugly, which it did in the past, he'd never become a monster.

She only looked human until she changed.

Then, there was no denying she was a monster.

But he didn't care. Eventually, neither did she, until Josephine came along.

The question wasn't would she be what Veronique was, but rather how soon. Now it was apparent; it would happen a lot sooner than she thought. She shuddered.

Seeming to sense this, Wall's arm worked its way around Veronique's shoulder. He squeezed her in his sleep and she rested her head back onto his chest.

Sometimes, he made her angry with his insistence of how he looked at her, how he loved her so fiercely. It wasn't natural. This thought made her mad, because *she* wasn't really natural either. Still, she wasn't capable of being angry at him for too long. She listened to his heart and fell asleep, letting her worries drift away for the time being.

***

The morning found Veronique in bed alone. Wall, always the early riser, had probably been awake for at least an hour, tending to the horses. She wouldn't see him until breakfast, which was a time coming soon.

She sat up and stretched. She saw the sun peeking up over the horizon through the bedroom window. It was time to wake up Josephine if she wasn't already awake.

She had an inner clock like her Daddy, which meant if she weren't in her room, she might very well be with him and the horses.

This never failed to make her smile.

Josephine was not like most little girls. Veronique had tried in vain to shower her with dolls and doll houses that she loved as a little girl.

Josephine didn't like them very much, until she began to play Rangers and Fugitives with the dolls. She didn't want to wear dresses, or frilly things. She wanted a gun. She wanted to ride horses. She wanted to be like her Daddy until she discovered that her Momma had been a sheriff.

That was all she could talk about for months.

Veronique never questioned her love for adventure. Who was she to tell her it wasn't lady like? Besides, Wall adored his little girl and never once tried to steer Josephine to dolls and such. Wall would have been uncomfortable playing dolls with her, but he loved playing bad and good guys with the dolls. Veronique would spends hours watching the two of them.

He was happier teaching her how to shoot though, and so was Josephine.

By the age of five, Josephine could take apart a gun, clean it and put it back together easily. She was a very good shot as well. She was one tough little cookie as her Daddy often told her.

Veronique put on her robe and walked to Josephine's room to find her sitting on the floor, talking to something she couldn't see.

"Well, that's pretty interesting," Josephine said. "How does it taste?"

There was silence, but Veronique felt a little buzzing in her head. The buzzing stopped. And Josephine began to speak again.

"Really? That's too bad." She said to nothing.

"Who are you talking to Jo?" Veronique asked.

Josephine turned and looked up at her mother, smiling.

"I made a little friend." She replied and held up her hand.

In her little palm was a yellow and black spider about two inches long.

Veronique blinked and looked again. The spider simply sat there.

"Say hi to my Momma," Josephine said, and the little buzzing rang in Veronique's head again. She didn't know what was happening, but it didn't feel wrong in some way.

"Um, hello," Veronique said, not wishing to startle the child.

The buzzing returned briefly and was quiet.

"She says you're very pretty." Josephine said.

"Well," Veronique began. "She is...a very pretty spider. Why don't you put her down and we can get breakfast ready for Daddy?"

"Okay," Josephine said and put the spider on the floor. "Don't worry, I won't step on you. And I'll talk to my Daddy."

Veronique heard the buzzing again and then stopped as the spider scurried under Josephine's bed.

Josephine stood up and ran to her Momma, hugging her tightly.

"Good mornin' Momma!" she said.

Veronique hugged her back, more than a little confused.

"Good morning, angel." She said, looking where the spider had been.

CHAPTER 3

Odessa, Texas 1895

In the three days that followed the incident at the Goshen Saloon, there was speculation that a bounty hunter would be hired to track down Stephan Trask. When no hunters could be found willing to take the case, a telegraphed message to the Governor from the Mayor had provided two Rangers. Still, there wasn't much of a guarantee that the Rangers would do much, but two law men had been assaulted, one killed in front of about fifteen witnesses.

Corporals Bob McCall and Henry Robb arrived early on the third day to visit see the Mayor, who was furious at the whole incident.

They were led into the Mayor's office by his secretary.

"Thanks, June." Mayor Johnson said, standing up and greeting the two Rangers. "Shut that door on the way out please."

The door closed and the Mayor shook hands with the men.

"Glad to see you boys," Johnson said. "This is one hell of a thing here."

"Why don't you tell us what happened?" McCall said.

Johnson told them what had happened with as much detail from the witnesses had given him. The two corporals nodded and listened. When the Mayor's story was done, McCall and Robb said nothing.

"Well?" Johnson said. "Nothing to say?"

"I'm gonna be honest with you, Mr. Mayor." Robb began. "If it were anybody but you tellin' us that story, I'd say they was full of shit."

Johnson blinked.

"Or drunker 'n hell." McCall added. "How does a man shove a goddamn gun barrel though a man's head? I mean, I've seen some things, but I'd be damned if that were even possible. Were all these folks drunk, tellin' you this story?"

"They most certainly were not!" Johnson said. "Look, I didn't call the Governor for you to tell me this story is strange. I know it's strange, but I got fifteen witnesses and a busted up sheriff telling me it's a goddamn fact. Not to mention a deputy with a damn gun in his head."

McCall looked at Robb. Neither of them had wanted to see what that looked like even though they knew they'd eventually have to.

"Can we see the sheriff?" McCall asked. "I'd sure feel a whole lot better about this if he can tell us something."

The Mayor nodded and grabbed his coat.

The three men left the office and walked down the street to where the sheriff had been laid up.

When they arrived at the doctor's office, the sheriff had been wrapped up tightly, both legs propped up and his head wrapped in cloth. He looked like a pile of busted timber.

The doctor warned about over exciting the sheriff, saying that he'd had nearly every bone in his body broken including a fractured skull.

"He gonna be able to talk?" Robb asked.

"Oh, he'll talk," the doctor said. "Bunch of incoherencies for the most part."

Robb had no idea what "incoherencies" meant, but he figured it wasn't good.

"Sheriff Williams?" the doctor said, leaning down to talk. "These here are Texas Rangers. They wanna ask you a few questions if that's alright."

The sheriff nodded.

"Sheriff, I know you're in a lot of pain, but can you tell me exactly what happened?" McCall asked.

The sheriff cleared his throat and winced.

"That goddamned Trask," he said. "Snapped off my hand at the wrist. Tossed me through the goddamned window like it were nothin'. Gonna put a bullet in his skull when I get out of here."

McCall saw how painful it was for him to speak and couldn't doubt the truth of what he had said.

"Sheriff, did he have anybody helping him that night?" Robb asked. "Anybody you didn't see maybe?"

"No, goddamn it." He replied. "Happened real fast, but weren't no one else with him that night. Son of a bitch..." He began to cough violently.

"I think that's enough for one day, boys." The doctor said as the sheriff began to flail. "Show yourselves out please, I'll be right with you."

The two Rangers looked stunned and walked out of the office. In the street, the just looked at each other.

"This is the damnedest thing I ever heard," Robb said.

McCall nodded.

"That's for sure.

Robb spit on the street and said.

"Where'd the witnesses say he was headed?"

"Corpus Christi," McCall said. "But I don't know if he was lying about that or what. Why the hell would you tell a bar full of witnesses where you was headed? With a stolen horse to boot?"

"We got anyone between here and there?"

"Not that I can think of," McCall rubbed his chin. "I think I heard Tom Wall was around Corpus Christi a few years back."

Robb nodded.

"Yeah, but he's retired damn near ten years now. Was a bounty hunter but I heard he even quit that. Got married or some damn thing."

"Think we ought to give him a head's up or something?"

Robb nodded.

"It couldn't hurt I reckon. He was a damn good Ranger."

"Damn true," McCall said. "Hell of a shot."

The doctor came out of the office and walked to the two men.

"The mayor's trying to keep him calm now, but I don't think it would be a good idea to talk to him again today." He said.

The two Rangers nodded.

"Doc, you reckon we can see the deputy?" McCall asked.

The Doc shuddered.

"Took me damn near three hours to get that gun out of his head," he said. "Other than the hole, ain't much to see."

"Well I guess we can skip that," Robb said.

"Thanks, doc." McCall said, shaking his hand. "I think we got enough right now."

The two man left the doctor and walked back to the mayor's office.

"Well, so we just send this Wall feller a telegram and call it a day?" McCall asked.

"I reckon we should start making our way to Corpus Christi as well." Robb said. "If this Trask is that dangerous, he's bound to make more messes on his way there. We might get lucky and head him off."

"Or we might get real damn unlucky and find him." added McCall. Robb nodded.

It was always a possibility.

**

After breakfast, Wall took a trip into town to see about any new orders for horses. He liked his new line of work of raising horses and he found he was quite good at it. He'd managed to make quite a good job of it and he was thankful. He wouldn't have to hunt anyone down for the rest of his life if he kept this up, and he was happy.

However, the bad feeling from a few evenings back managed to stick in his craw longer than he had intended. He had tried pushing it out of his mind, but he'd had too many feelings like that wind up happening than not. He'd have to own up to it eventually, but today didn't feel like the day.

Today, he was Tom Wall, husband, father and rancher. That suited him just fine.

He rode into the town proper on his favorite horse Haystack. Hay, as he was called, was a very stocky horse that had been up for auction a few years back. Wall didn't have the heart to see the horse sold for meat, so he bought it and rode it home. The horse seemed to always be grateful somehow for it and had been Wall's constant companion ever since.

He thought about Veronique and how worried she was; she seemed to always be worried about something. He was pretty good at calming her down, but it was getting harder as Josephine was getting older and showing signs of being like her mother.

Wall was very concerned, but he learned a long time ago that it was a waste of time to worry about things you couldn't change. His wife and daughter were two of them. Not that he wanted them to be different. More than anything, he wanted Veronique to quit worrying about it. He couldn't do anything but assure her that things would be okay, even if he had no idea how he could make good on that promise.

The only thing he could do was just love them as hard as he could and hope to hell it was enough.

Wall rode up to the import stables near the Givens grocery and put Haystack in front of the water trough. He patted him on his flank and walked into the stables.

"Why, young mister Tom," called out Paul Brine. Brine was the owner of the stables and impossibly old to boot. Wall had slowly become his favorite customer. Brine walked slowly over to him smiling with a mouth of missing teeth. "What brings here today?"

"Just seein' if there's any new horses." Wall said, shaking the old man's hand. "How you feeling, Pop?"

Wall was about the only person to get away with calling Brine "Pop." Anyone else would get an earful.

"Ah, I'm feeling finer than frog's hair split four ways," Brine said, chuckling. Wall laughed as well.

"I guess that's pretty good," Wall said.

"How's that house full o' beauties you got out there Tom?"

"Oh, they're doing just fine. Said to say hi." Wall said. "The missus said she'll be making her buttermilk pies in another week or two. I think she told me to tell you just to get your mouth waterin',"

Brine smiled. It was his favorite pie in a world where pies were damn near everywhere in town.

"Ah, bless that woman's heart," he said. "If you hadn't married that woman, I'd be a courtin' her."

"I bet you would at that," Wall said.

"Well son, I hate to tell you, but ain't nothing rolling in for you for a while." Brine said. "I'll keep my eyes open for you though. Maybe you and the ladies ought to go take a little rest somewhere. Y'all ain't to far from the sea. Bet the little one would love that,"

Brine had a point. Maybe a day or two out by the ocean wouldn't be such a bad idea.

"Might be a good idea," He said.

"Ya damn right," Brine said.

"Well, I reckon I'll go see about picking up a few things for the missus. I'll see ya, Pop."

"Say hi to them girls," Brine said and walked back to his chair in the back of the stables.

Wall walked out and over to Givens grocery. It wasn't a huge store, but it was just fine for Wall's little family.

He opened the door and a little bell sounded. Melissa Givens, the owner's wife called out from the back of the store.

"With you in a flash!" she said in a high lilted voice. She was from Georgia originally and had retained the accent.

Wall began to look around. He didn't need anything really, but he liked to get little things for Veronique and Josephine when he could. He had money these days; a lot more than he'd ever thought he'd have in his whole life. He didn't even really need to work, but he wasn't afraid of hard work and he would be bored out of his mind if he quit doing things.

He worked for himself, and that suited him just fine. That meant he wouldn't have to quit.

He heard footsteps and saw Melissa pop into view.

"Well, I declare! Mr. Wall!" she said, "How you doin' sugar? Where are those ladies of yours?"

Wall nodded and smiled. She was a very nice lady, but she always managed to make him feel uncomfortable for some reason.

"The girls are good, ma'am," he said.

"I'm so very glad to hear that," she cooed. "Now, what can I do you for today?"

"Just lookin' around," he said. "Anything new?"

"Well, as a matter of fact I have something that came in early this morning just for you. Picked it up at the Post Office. I was gonna run it over to you folks."

Wall's eyebrows raised.

"What's that?" he asked.

"You got a telegraphed message from Odessa, Mr. Wall. Looks...*official*." she said, her eyes beaming.

She went behind the counter and picked up an envelope. She gingerly handed it to Wall, who tore it open slowly.

He began to read, frowning the whole time.

THE WESTERN UNION TELEGRAPH COMPANY

TO: CAPT. TOMAS WALL (RET) FROM: CPL.
     R. MCCALL

RE: FUGITIVE HEADED YOUR WAY. STEPHAN
     TRASK CRIPPLED ODESSA SHERIFF
     KILLED DEPUTY STOLE HORSE. CLAIMED
     HEADED TO CORPUS CHRISTI. ME AND

```
PARTNER IN PURSUIT. WANTED TO GIVE
YOU  WARNING.  ANY  HELP  WELCOME.
SHOULD BE NEARER TO YOU IN 10 DAYS.
VERY DANGEROUS. BOB MCCALL
```

Wall read it a few times. He was concerned of course, but mainly he was wondering how anyone outside of Corpus Christi knew where he was in the first place.

Not that he was exactly hiding, but he sure as hell wasn't advertising where he was either. McCall was a good man, so it wasn't his fault he knew where to find him, but someone had opened their mouth and that was not good.

He read it one more time.

"Well?" Melissa Givens asked. "What's it say?"

"I need to go talk to Clancy," he said and walked out the door.

***

Sheriff Clancy O'Hare was a very large man and was very much feared in Corpus Christi. He had been one of the first Irish lawmen in Texas and did not take it lightly.

He was fair, but incredibly tough. He did not tolerate a foolish man and he made sure to let everyone know that. Whether you liked him or not, one thing was sure; he was feared by most.

Except by Tom Wall.

Clancy appreciated Wall and respected him. He also liked the young man quite a bit as he had helped him a few times during some rough spots a few years back. He was pleased to see Wall come through his door, but that didn't last as he saw the look on his face.

"Tommy, me lad, you look like someone pissed in yer whisky," Clancy said.

"Look at this," Wall said, handing the still seated Clancy the telegraph. Clancy read it and sighed.

"Ya think they'd send it ta the feckin sheriff," Clancy said. He put the telegraph down and looked up at Wall. "Well? What are ye planning?"

Wall took a seat on the opposite side of Clancy's big desk.

"I ain't sure yet," Wall said. "I figured you ought to know what's coming and I figured I'd ask you what you thought about it."

Clancy smiled. He liked being respected.

"Nice to have a little professional courtesy, Tommy. As one constable to another, I'm open to suggestions. You're the one with more experience with these sort o' folks."

Wall was always amused whenever Clancy would call him "constable." It certainly sounded like it commanded respect.

"My first inclination is to try and head him off," Wall said. "But, I ain't a ranger or a bounty hunter anymore. Never mind constable."

Clancy smirked.

"Then why do you look so damn excited?"

Wall had to admit, if only to himself, that the prospect of riding out to meet Trask had been appealing if only to his ego.

"I'm a family man now, Clanc." Wall said, ignoring the statement. "I can't be roamin' all over hell's creation anymore."

"Not even if you want to, eh?" Clancy said still smirking.

At this, Wall smirked too.

"If you were in my seat," Clancy continued. "What would you do? A proper sheriff wouldn't leave town. So, what would you do?"

"I ain't the sheriff," Wall said, but he was thinking. "But, there ain't too much you can do. You just have to wait and see if and when he shows up. About ten days or so according to the message. That being said, I'd clean up the shotguns."

Clancy laughed.

"Smart man, Tommy."

"It's kept me alive so far I guess."

"So far, so good." Clancy knocked on his wooden desk for luck.

Wall looked at the sheriff. Clancy didn't look worried, but he did look concerned.

"Look, I know those two rangers. Good men. If anyone's got a shot at stopping this feller, it's them two. Hell, we might never set eyes on him."

"See? You're a lot more resourceful than I'll ever be, Tommy."

Wall smiled.

"I'm heading over to the Post Office. Any messages?" Wall asked.

"You tell that goddamn limey Pratt to shake his arse over here if he's got any more messages." Clancy said. His beef with Terrence Pratt was near legendary.

"Hell, he gave my message to Miss Givens,"

"Jesus on a pinwheel," Clancy sighed. "That woman needs to leave that goddamn Pratt alone. Ought to haul them both in,"

Wall laughed, and knocked on the desk on his way out.

"Thanks, Tommy." Clancy said.

***

While Wall walked to the Post Office, it bothered him slightly that he wasn't going full blast after Trask and tried to keep his cool about it.

He hadn't been this riled up in a long time and he wondered why.

But, it was for the best he reckoned. He had responsibilities.

Still, Trask sounded like a challenge, and Wall hadn't had this kind of challenge in years. Sure, the last one damn near killed him and Veronique...

But damn, it had been fun in a way.

He'd talk to Veronique about it later. Maybe he'd head back to Givens' after all and buy her something pretty. It might keep her from yelling at him in one of the five different languages she knew.

Although, he kind of liked that too.

He sighed.

CHAPTER 4

San Angelo, TX

Sancho's Billiards wasn't a very good brothel, even by San Angelo standards. The whores were ugly and mean, the liquor was watered down mercilessly and the entire place was filthy. The only good thing about it actually, was that it was cheap and the only billiards room in town at the moment.

There had been more, of course. Three to be exact, but they had all mysteriously caught fire in the same week a year ago. Folks knew it had been Shifty Packer, the owner of Sancho's, but all were too afraid of him to do anything about it. And that, of course, suited Shifty just fine.

Trask rode in and tied his horse right in front of Sancho's hoping for a whore and a game of cards. For some reason, even when the town had four brothels, he always chose Sancho's. Although he was a very well kept man, he preferred the filth of this place.

He walked in and over to the bar. The barkeep, a sad, thin man shuffled over to him. He had horrible acne and greasy black hair. He appeared to have a very bad lazy eye which threw off Trask for a moment.

"Drink, senior?" he asked in a high accented voice.

"Cervaza," Trask said.

"No cerveza, senior."

"What do you have?"

"Whisky, tequila."

"Whisky then, por favor."

The barkeep reached down and pulled up a shot glass and a bottle. He sloshed some light colored whisky into the glass and pushed it to Trask.

"Gracias," Trask mumbled as he lifted the dirty shot glass to his mouth. He knocked it back, grimaced and slammed the glass down.

He looked at the barkeep as if he had done some great disservice to him and then looked away.

"Where's Shifty?" he asked.

The barkeep cleared his throat in an appalling manner.

"Upstairs," came the reply.

"Go get him, por favor."

"Right now?" the barkeep asked, sounding a little annoyed.

Trask slowly turned towards him and looked him in the eye. He didn't say a word, but the barkeep understood. He quickly walked from behind the bar and ran up the stairs.

Trask looked around the place. It had actually gotten filthier. It was so unsavory, the black beetles that usually scurried around on the floor weren't there. If they were, he couldn't see them as some sort of black thing now covered…or stuck…to the floor.

He smiled.

He heard movement upstairs and a loud crash. The barkeep stumbled back down the stairs, bleeding from his left eye.

He staggered behind the bar and walked up to Trask.

"He said he's not here,"

Trask looked at the bar and sighed.

"What room is he not in?" he asked.

The barkeep had to think before answering this question and decided that this gringo could do a lot worse the punch him in his eye.

"Four," he replied sheepishly.

"Thanks," Trask said and walked to the staircase. As he climbed the stairs, he heard commotion from where room four probably housed Shifty. He put his hand on his gun, just as a precaution and waited at the top of the stairs.

The door marked four burst open, and Shifty, stark naked and holding a sawed off shot gun jumped into the hallway. He had Trask dead to rights and for a moment, he held his gaze. He blinked repeatedly as Trask began to laugh.

Shifty frowned, then smiled, slowly lowering his shotgun.

"You damn near got your ass blowed off," he said.

"You would have missed," Trask said. "And I would have shot *your* pecker off."

"I appreciate your restraint." Shifty held his shotgun in front of his genitalia. It didn't hide anything.

"Your luck, it woulda just grown back, bigger than ever."

Shifty laughed hard.

"Let me throw on some pants, Amigo. I'll be right down."

"Fair enough," Trask said, already heading back down the stairs. The few people in the brothel were not only shocked that Trask had in fact not been blown off of his feet, but that they had all just heard Shifty laugh. They watched Trask make it all the way to the bottom of the stairs and then to the bar without a mark on him. This could mean only one thing.

This man was more dangerous than Shifty.

A few minutes passed and Shifty bounded down the stairs in a pair of dirty pants, boots and an unbuttoned shirt. He held a smile that was terrifying because it was genuine. Shifty only smiled when he was going to kill someone. To see it on display like that, without him firing a gun at anyone scared them all. It was new. Unpredictable.

He sidled up to Trask and nearly clapped him on the back. He thought better of it and just pulled up next to him.

"What brings you to this shithole, amigo?" Shifty asked. "Runnin'?"

"You know me better than that," Trask picked up the bottle of whisky and poured a shot. He slid it over to Shifty. "I don't run. I just don't linger."

Both men laughed. Shifty lifted his shot glass to Trask, and Trask lifted the bottle. Both men drank. Shifty's face twisted into one of nausea.

"Paco, you fuck!" he yelled to the barkeep. "Bring me my whisky, goddamn it!" He spit on the floor to make his point. He leaned over to Trask. "Apologies," he said.

Trask nodded.

"No need for special treatment," he said. "But I do have a favor to ask if you don't mind."

"Name it," Shifty said.

Trask leaned in.

"When was the last time you killed a law man?"

Shifty smiled.

"Been too long. Why?"

"There's probably gonna be a couple coming your way looking for me."

"What did you do?"

Trask pulled on the whisky bottle.

"Killed a law man," he said.

Shifty chuckled.

"Crippled the sheriff to boot." Trask added.

"Crippled? Not bad. Surprised he's still alive."

"Been working on my personality more," Trask said. "Didn't even mean to cripple the bastard. Hell, didn't even mean to kill the deputy. Just bad timing is all."

Shifty looked at him and nodded.

"So, you want me to cover for you if they send someone after you?"

"No," Trask began. "I want you to flat out kill anyone looking for me. I ain't playing this time, Shifty. I ain't got the time to be chased down like a common horse thief."

"You stole a goddamn horse too?" Shifty shook his head. "No shame at all. What the hell's gotten into you?"

"I had to get out of town. My horse was clear on the other side of Odessa." Trask took another drink. "I mean, Jesus, what would *you* have done?"

"I'd have killed the goddamn sheriff for one thing," Shifty said. Paco, the barkeep, came over with a darker bottle of whisky. Shifty grunted something and Paco left quickly. He pulled the cork and took a long pull on the whisky. He offered the bottle to Trask, who took it gladly.

"That's good," Trask said. "And to be fair, I didn't think the sheriff would have lived."

"Ah, what the hell can you do, right? Don't worry, *Amigo*. I'll see what I can do."

***

Wall walked on to the porch with two pretty bonnets in his hands; one for Veronique and one for Josephine. Except, of course, Josephine's bonnet wasn't a bonnet as much as it was a cowboy's hat her size. He knew she wouldn't wear a bonnet, and he'd already blown enough money on a half closet full of bonnets that would have to wait for a granddaughter.

He figured he could wait a long damn time for that to happen.

Before he reached the door, Veronique opened it and met him. The look on her face was one of concern.

"She talks to spiders," she said.

Wall smiled.

"Well hell, darling. I just got done talkin' to the horse. All the damn way home."

She shook her head.

"Your horse doesn't talk back,"

"Of course he don't," he said. He was about to say something else until what she had said hit him.

"They talk *back?*"

She nodded.

"Well," he said, shifting his gait. "What do they *say?*"

"I don't know. I can hear them buzzing, but not any words. This is not something I'm able to do, Tom."

"Is she scared?"

"Of course not," Veronique said, sitting on the little porch glider. "She's not afraid of *anything.* I'm terrified."

"Why?" Tom sat down next to her, letting the bonnet and hat drop on the porch.

"*Why?*" Veronique sounded surprised at this. "I just told you our daughter talks with spiders. *Spiders*, Tom."

"Well now, hold on a minute, darlin'. She has somewhat of an *interesting* combination of things going on in her. We both knew she was going to be different."

"But, this is a different that I *don't know how to handle.* This isn't something I can do. What if there's more?"

Wall grabbed her hand.

"Then we do our best." He said. "We try to not look scared and we damn sure try not to scare her. This is who *she* is, right?"

"I was turned into this when I was eleven," Veronique said. "I didn't have a choice in it."

Tom considered this for a moment.

"Well, I have this one eyebrow. Left one. Bigger than the other one. Always made me look like I was real interested in what people had to say even if I weren't. Apart from you, I don't find much interest in what most people have to say."

Veronique looked at him dumbfounded.

He smirked.

"What I'm sayin' is, you didn't have a choice, Josephine doesn't either and neither do I. We got what we got." He shrugged his shoulders. "I reckon it's what we do with it that counts."

A small smile broke out on her face.

"I always liked that eyebrow," she said.

"It likes you too."

She sighed and kissed his hand.

"How are you so calm all the time? Don't you worry?"

Wall kissed her hand.

"What do I got to worry about?" he said. "Besides, if Josephine can talk to spiders, maybe she can get them to stay the hell out of my boots."

She couldn't help it. She laughed and nearly cackled. She squeezed his hand tightly.

"Oh, Tom." She said. "It was scary, but I have to admit. She did look adorable talking to the spider."

"She looks adorable pretty much doing anything, Mrs. Wall. Just like her Momma."

Her smile darkened into a sad frown.

"She's just going to keep changing," she said. "She's developing things I've never even heard of and I don't know that I'll be able to help her."

"Who helped you?" Wall asked. "You said you were turned into...well, you. Were you shown what to do?"

Veronique shuddered.

"The man who turned me killed my family in front of me. Made me..." She suddenly stopped.

"Made you what?"

She took a deep breath.

"*Feed*."

This was something she had never told him and he felt a chill stab him hard in his spine.

"Jesus," was all he could say.

She shook her head.

"Jesus had nothing to do with this," she said angrily.

They sat together, holding hands and looking at each other until finally Wall spoke.

"That ain't going to happen this time, darlin'."

She smiled weakly.

"But, I won't know what to do."

"We're parents," he said. "Ain't never known one who did know what the hell to do. We'll just do what we think is best and love the little sprite as best we can. It's all we got."

"We're not regular parents," Veronique said.

"No, we *are*. At the end of the day, that's what we are to that one little girl in there, and that's the best thing in the world. She don't know about being poor, or missing a mother or father. We are the world right now for her, and for her, our whole job is to be the best damn world, cos ain't no one else gonna do it the way we can."

She looked at him long and then kissed him longer.

"I love you Tom Wall,"

"I love you too,"

"You know, she's asleep right now."

Wall's eyebrows raised.

"That a fact?"

"Indeed it is."

"Well," Wall said standing up. "I'll give you your hat later then."

"Hat?"

"Trust me," he said, pulling her towards him as she stood. "You're gonna want to wait for the hat."

CHAPTER 5

San Angelo, Texas

"If you don't stop killing my whores, I'm going to be a little pissed off, amigo." Shifty said as Trask walked down the brothel's steps with a

"She's probably not dead," he said, laying her across the top of the bar. Shifty walked over and took a look at her face.

He spit on the floor behind the bar.

"Goddamn it, Trask."

Trask shrugged his shoulders.

"I'll take her out back," he said, pulling the girl off of the bar and back onto his shoulder.

"Put her in the kitchen," Shifty said. "I got an idea. But no more goddamn whores for you."

"Yeah," Trask said through his teeth and walked into the kitchen. There was a loud crash. Someone screamed something in Spanish in the kitchen which was met with a loud slap and a louder thud. A moment later, Trask burst through the door.

"You been here one whole day," Shifty said. He was furious, but he chose his words very carefully. "And you killed three whores."

"Three ugly whores," Trask said. "And when did you start caring about their well-being?"

"Three of five ugly whores and now, two ugly whores."

"Didn't think you knew math,"

Shifty looked at Trask and saw that he was already looking back at him.

Shifty forced a smile and pretended to laugh.

"Nice, Trask." He said, chuckling. He looked at him for a moment longer, turned and walked away.

"I know you're afraid of me," Trask said. "You tolerate me because you know I'll kill you just to look at you, right?"

Shifty stopped in his tracks.

"And you also know that I'm smarter than you. You've been kidding yourself thinking I'm some kind of friend."

Shifty turned around to face Trask.

"I'm the one tolerating you," Trask said.

Shifty smiled. He was petrified, but he wasn't exactly a coward either.

"Whatever you say Trask," he said. "But I also know what it is you are. Known for a good long while too. Something happens to me, and other folks will know it too."

Trask blinked a few times and then smiled.

"Who the hell would believe you and more importantly, who'd give a single fuck if I killed you?"

"That's the fun part," Shifty said. "The message that goes out after I die also includes how to kill you."

"And how the hell would you know how to do that?"

"Wanna try me, amigo?"

"Mexican standoff," Trask said. He clapped his hands three times. "Maybe I do like you a little bit, Shifty. Just don't push me too hard."

"No more killing my whores," Shifty said, adding "Please."

Trask nodded and walked back upstairs. When he heard the room door slam shut, Shifty slumped and began to hyperventilate. He knew how close he was to dying just then and he had made it.

Running this whorehouse was starting to turn into work.

He walked into the kitchen to see if Trask had killed his goddamn cook as well. If he had, then he figured he'd have more ingredients for his new idea.

***

Josephine woke up from her nap, frowning. She'd had a dream that her new spider friend had taken them on a wonderful adventure. The spider's name had turned out to be Pajkov, which was sort of a weird name she thought. But, not everyone talks to spiders she also thought.

Josephine and Pajkov went to the ocean. She had to hold him because he was tiny and couldn't walk on the sand very well. They found a chunk of driftwood and Josephine rinsed it off in the water so Paj could walk on it.

The two new friends talked and laughed. It was a good dream.

Until someone else showed up in her dream.

She couldn't see his face, but she knew it was a man. He was in head to toe black clothes and he almost seemed to not be walking on the sand but above it. He slowly came towards them. Pajkov told Josephine to run, but Josephine didn't want to run. She wanted to see who it was.

"No, you don't," Pajkov said. "He's dangerous."

"I don't run," she said. She wasn't trying to sound tough, but she was scared.

"I'll protect you as much as I can," Pajkov said. With that, Pajkov began to change. The spider began to grow massive and though he didn't change in appearance, his more deadly features became easier to see.

Josephine watched as Pajkov scamper (*thundered*) down the beach to intercept the dark figure and that was when she woke up.

She wasn't afraid, but she was confused. She hopped out of bed and looked around her room for her spider friend. He wasn't to be found.

She stepped out of her room and walked past the room where her parents slept. She heard her Daddy snoring lightly. She tiptoed to the front door. She wasn't allowed off of the porch, but she didn't need to go off of it for where she was going.

She gently closed the front door behind her and walked to the far right of the porch.

Her mother's daffodils.

She smiled. They had become her favorite flower and her mother had planted a lot of them. She leaned over the little rail and looked down. It was late in the afternoon, but the sun was still bright and she could see the little bugs flying and crawling around.

And the spiders.

She didn't see Pajkov, but she saw several other ones.

"Do any of y'all know where Pajkov is?" she asked.

The spiders sat on their webs and didn't move.

"Can you hear me?"

Still, nothing.

"Why can I only talk to him? Can't none of you hear me?"

One of the larger spiders moved on its web and turned facing Josephine's direction.

"How do you speak to us?" it asked. Its voice sounded like buzzing.

"Well, how do you speak back?" she asked back.

"We are *all* Pajkov," it said.

Josephine thought about this, but it didn't make any sense to her.

The spider turned its back on Josephine and returned to its original position. She frowned.

"Rude," she said and turned her attentions elsewhere.

CHAPTER 6

Corpus Christi, Texas

Wall got out of bed as Veronique slept quietly. He threw on his pants and shirt. He looked out of the window and figured the sun put the day around four. He didn't want to wake her up just to have her cook dinner. A small, rare smile broke out on his face as he figured he could take his girls into town for the evening.

Corpus Christi proper boasted a restaurant that had all sorts of goodies on the menu. He loved his wife's cooking most times, but it was a rare thing to get almost exactly what you want. He chuckled a little bit.

"Have I put you in a cheerful mood?" Veronique said in a sleepy voice.

He turned and looked at his sleepy smiling wife.

"Judgin' from that look on your face, seemed to have worked both ways."

"What time is it?" she asked.

"About four. How 'bout I take my favorite ladies into town for a nice dinner?"

Veronique, always practical began to protest, but she really couldn't think of a good reason against it.

"I am not in the mood to argue with you, Tom. That sounds lovely. Where's Josephine?"

"I'll go get her," he said, putting on his boots. "Probably all covered in mud somewhere. I'll toss her in the creek real quick."

This made Veronique laugh.

"She can wash herself, never mind you tossing her into the creek."

He started to walk out of the bedroom.

"One day, she's gonna be too big to toss anywhere," he said. He turned and smiled. "Gotta get my child tossing in where I can."

He left the room and went to find his daughter.

***

The entire Wall family sat in Fisher's Restaurant, all dressed up for a lovely family dinner. Wall had found his daughter, of course, covered in mud as he thought and indeed, tossed her into the river with great delight. He then lugged her home to get her dressed up for the evening.

Fisher's was the only restaurant in miles of Corpus Christie, and it was very simple. Lamp lit, quiet except for the kitchen and one meal served a day. It wasn't full of choice-it was usually steak since Verne Fisher owned most of the cattle in Corpus Christie. There was also a vast supply of canned green beans.

It was a mundane place to eat unless you absolutely loved meat.

Wall hadn't had much of a taste for meat that he didn't carve his own self these days, but he reckoned that maybe he'd give it a try if his ladies were willing. Veronique seemed to sense this and put a hand on his.

"Tom, its cow." She said quietly. "If it were anything else I'd tell you."

Wall looked at her and smirked.

"I reckon you'd know." He said.

She smiled back.

"What are you and Daddy talkin' about?" Josephine said. She was a little fidgety in her dress. It's not that she disliked dresses, but she liked not wearing them more.

"Nothin' darlin'." Wall said. "I heard they got buttermilk pie here."

Josephine's eyes grew. If there was one thing in the whole world that Josephine loved more than getting covered in mud and playing Ranger with her father, it was, buttermilk pie. In fact, this was a trait shared by both daughter and father. Veronique had practiced making the pie special for both of them although she couldn't stand it herself.

"Can I just have that?" Josephine asked and Veronique snorted a laugh.

"Just like your father," she said. "And no, you cannot just have *that.*"

Both daughter and father looked disappointed.

"And you'll *both* need your vegetables." Veronique added.

This time, Wall protested.

"Now wait a minute here," he said, trying not to laugh. "I take you girls down to this here fine eatery so there ain't no dishes or mess at home and you're gonna make us eat vegetables *anyway*?"

Veronique smiled and said,

"I most certainly am, my love. And do you know why?"

"Because you love us," Josephine said. She was sincere but not very excited about it either.

"That's correct, little one." She said.

"Just don't seem right is all," Wall said, still trying to not laugh.

"If both of my darlings want to have buttermilk pie," Veronique said. "Then you will *both* have your greens. Period."

Wall leaned over to Josephine conspiratorially.

"I reckon I can eat my greens quicker than you,"

Josephine looked him square in the eye.

"You're on." She replied.

Mrs. Fisher came over with water and milk for Josephine. She took their orders and went back to the kitchen. The family sat, talking about family things.

The door to the restaurant opened and in walked Clancy, with a furrowed look on his face. He walked directly to Wall's table, removing his hat.

"Tommy, ladies," Clancy said.

"Clancy," Wall said, his face darkening. "You don't look so happy. There a problem?"

"Can I talk to you outside Tommy? It's a bit sensitive. Won't take up too much of yer time,"

Wall looked at Veronique and she nodded.

"'Scuse me," Wall said standing up. "Be right back,"

Clancy led Wall to the front porch of the restaurant. He leaned in close.

"That bloke, Trask? Just got word from San Angelo that he's there. Looks like he's set up there at some whorehouse. Doesn't look like he's in any rush to leave, but he's closer than he was." Clancy said. Wall just looked at him.

"That it?" Wall asked.

"Isn't that enough?" came the reply. "That's one rough town, full o' unsavory bastards, that place. Might be trying to put together somethin'."

Wall rubbed his chin.

"I ain't sure what you're getting' at Clancy. I know you're trying to tell me something,"

Clancy's face darkened.

"Goddamn it, man. He's comin' here."

"You don't know that, Clancy." Wall said. "There ain't no way to know that for sure."

"I feel it in my guts, son." Clancy said and put a hand on Wall's shoulder. "You know as well as I do that you have to trust these things. I don't want to cause an upheaval in your little family, but you may want to clean your guns."

Wall swallowed. Clancy may be right, but Wall couldn't tell what his guts felt. Still, he trusted Clancy and nodded.

"I may just do that, Clancy." He said finally.

"Look, go eat. Enjoy the night, but I'm tellin' Boy-o, be ready."

Clancy clapped his shoulder twice and walked off.

Wall stood there for a few moments, considering what he'd need to do, and without a doubt, he needed to do something he didn't want to do.

He'd need to tell Veronique.

She wasn't a stranger to violence, but things were different now. Now, there was Josephine. It was too dangerous.

Still, she had been a sheriff and a pretty damn good one.

**

Wall, Veronique and Josephine had a wonderful dinner and some very good buttermilk pie. The came home and put Josephine in her bed. She was asleep before they walked out of her room.

Holding hands, Wall and Veronique stepped onto the porch and sat next to each other. They didn't say anything for a while, just held hands and enjoyed the silence.

"So, what is it you want to tell me, love?" Veronique asked.

"I ain't never had much of a good poker face have I?"

Veronique smiled.

"Not since I've known you,"

Wall sighed.

"Clancy got a telegram," he said. "There's this feller on his way here, or so he thinks. Pretty bad one at that. Killed a deputy, crippled the sheriff over in Odessa. Takin' his sweet time, but it looks like he's coming here. Asked me for help on it."

"I knew the sheriff in Odessa," she said. "He was a good man. Hard to think someone could hurt him that badly."

Wall nodded.

"So, when do you leave?"

"I don't know that I will leave," he said, looking at her. "If he ain't on his way here, I could be throwing myself into something I don't need to get involved with. I got you and the little one to think about anyway."

"I know you, Tom. You've probably already plotted something out haven't you?"

He shrugged.

"And since when have I been defenseless?" she added.

"Probably never," he said.

"Any idea who this man is?" she asked. "I used to get lots of wanted posters back in the day."

"Name's Trask. Stephen I think."

Veronique squeezed his hand.

"Stephan?"

"Yeah, that's it. Hey, do you..." Wall stopped and looked at his wife, who wore a look he'd only seen once before.

Fear.

"Who is he?" he asked.

"You...*can't* go after him." She said. "We need to leave."

She let go of his hand and stood up. He stood up as well.

"Now just a minute, who the hell is this man?"

She turned but he grabbed her arm.

"Darlin' I ain't foolin'. Ain't nobody spooks you like this." He turned her around. "Who is he?"

He looked in her face and saw the angry tears flowing freely. She opened her mouth to speak but no words came. She fell into his arms and he hugged her tightly as she sobbed.

"Let it out, darlin'," he said calmly. "Just let it out."

He stood there for a while just holding her, wondering who the hell in the world could scare his wife that badly.

CHAPTER 7

San Angelo Texas 1895

Stephan Trask lay in bed next to a woman whose name he couldn't remember. He was troubled. Not about the woman of course, but about her perception of him. That worried him.

In his younger days, he was vile and cruel. The reactions he'd gotten back then were understandable. He'd done vicious things without hesitation and thought. He'd killed his way across the country at least three times. He destroyed families, children entire settlements without a care. He was a terror to be sure.

And to be fair, they were right.

But after a couple of hundred years, he wasn't the same. He wasn't cruel. He wasn't violent. Far from it, he was a generous man who tried his best to fit in.

He had to survive, of course and tried to limit his feedings.

It was more difficult than he'd thought.

Even his small family had thought him a monster. A monster among monsters; the concept was both confusing and offensive.

The last time he'd seen Bosen, he'd come very close to killing him right on the docks of Trieste in Slovenia. Bosen had taken a small group of the family, including his beloved Viorica to flee to the new world. He swore he'd destroy Bosen if he ever saw him again.

After fuming about it, he decided that he'd try his fortunes in America too, and that, he discovered was an excellent idea.

The Mexicans called him *Diablo Vampiro*. The Chippewa mistook him for a Wendigo. He'd been called a lot of things but the one most often called was monster.

Everywhere, every time.

He was determined to be different, to not be a monster.

He'd nearly given up hope until he ran into Bosen.

Well, decades later, he'd run into Bosen and had welcomed him with open arms, much to the surprise of both men.

He had talked to Bosen and forgiven him for his betrayal. Bosen had told him of the town he had started in Arizona territory and Trask was not only impressed, but loved the idea. It meant that the monster could be a good thing and it would be safe to feed in such a manner.

But then Bosen told the story about the end of the town. The ranger who came from nowhere. The ranger his beloved Viorica had wanted to run off with and ruin everything. Except now, she wasn't Viorica.

She was called Veronique.

Trask questioned Bosen about her whereabouts, to which Bosen said he didn't know. He said he was going to find and kill her for her betrayal.

Trask understood the feeling. He was sympathetic. Hadn't he felt the same way about Bosen? Of course, he was benevolent.

But, who was Bosen to make a decision to kill her like that? Who was Bosen to decide the fate of one of their own? One of his own?

Insolence!

Bosen had been forgiven after all and then he betrayed him yet again. After wondering what to do, he left Bosen to rot on his own and began to look for Viorica on his own.

He'd kill him another time.

But, he had a different name now to help the hunt.

And Trask began the awful task of trying to find one man in a country of many. The man's name was Wall. There were books written about him and he read every one of them.

He hated Tom Wall.

Finally, he'd found the one penny dreadful that brought up his beloved.

And his heart sank.

She was called Veronique Wall now. She had been a sheriff (unheard of) and was now, this *human's* wife.

Wife.

Didn't he know he was inferior?

Apparently not.

And her.

So disappointed.

He grew angry thinking about this and he struggled to calm down.

He punched the woman next to him and instantly regretted it.

She'd been dead for hours and he had more respect for the dead than that, or so he believed.

He looked at her and kissed the nape of her neck, broken as it was.

Shifty was right, and perhaps it was time for him to move on after all. He'd wasted too much time. He finally knew where she was and more importantly, where he was going.

He was ready for his beloved.

He just hoped he'd learned to control himself before he accidentally killed her or something rash like that.

***

Trask looked at Shifty who had a small grin on his face.

"I'm afraid I won't see you again my friend." He said. "But thank you for putting up with me the past week. I know it isn't easy to be my friend, but know that you always are."

Trask hugged the man tightly and let him go.

Shifty's body slumped to the floor as Trask walked out, throwing a cigarillo on to the floor. The one bottle of whisky that was actually whisky had been spilled. The liquid caught on fire and quickly spread by the time Trask had reached his borrowed horse.

Shifty's body, which had been dead about two days now, caught fire as well. The brothel and all of its occupants might have been listed as the first victims in a freak fire that nearly consumed the entire town had Trask not killed everyone there.

There were still some things that Trask could not abide.

He silently asked forgiveness as he made his way toward Corpus Christi.

***

Wall held his sleeping wife on the porch for an hour before bringing her inside and into bed. When he had done that, he grabbed the wooden box from under the bed and brought it out onto the porch.

He grabbed a lit lantern and set it on its brightest wick setting. He opened the box and grabbed the tobacco pouch and papers that sat atop a cloth covering the rest of the box's contents.

It had been a few years, but he had rolled a cigarette and lit it in under a minute. He held the smoke in deeply and exhaled slowly.

He pulled off the cloth.

There were five wooden gun boxes, oil cloth, oil and bullets. Sitting on the top of the first box was his badge which said two things. One was TEXAS RANGER. The other was CAPTAIN.

He puffed on his cigarette and pulled the boxes out, setting them next to each other. In each box was a gun, and Wall pulled each one out, cleaned it, loaded it and put it back in the boxes.

The last gun was his father's gun. He cleaned it carefully, almost affectionately. He held it out in front of him and sighed. He didn't bother thinking about what his Pa would've done. He just missed him a whole lot at that moment. He lit another cigarette and held the gun on his lap.

By the time his smoke was done, he had put the guns back into their respective boxes. He'd have to get going before daybreak.

Before Veronique could talk him out of it.

This Trask fellow was responsible for a lot of things and he was going to have to pay for some of them. At least as much as Wall could dish out.

And he could dish out plenty even without the guns, no doubt, but this was a foe for which he wasn't fully prepared to face and he knew it.

The last time he faced one of Veronique's kind, it had taken intervention from her to save his life.

He sat back, considering this for a moment.

He would die if he went toe to toe with Trask. His job was to keep his family safe and he'd fail miserably if he faced him alone.

He had no idea what to do for the first time in his life.

"I know what you're thinking, lover." Veronique said from behind him.

He no longer questioned when she did things like simply appear without a sound. And if Trask did it, He'd be dead before he heard a thing.

"I don't know what to do to protect you and I can't just goddamn run away," he said.

She sat next to him quietly.

"I've never run from a thing in my whole life, darlin'." He continued. "And I ain't inclined to start now, but this is the first time I feel like we can't do nothin' *but* run."

"I don't know that we have a choice, Tom. He's powerful. And he's old. Older than me."

"What's that got to do with anything?"

"Age begets power," she said. "The older one of us gets, the stronger we become."

"But you can't live forever," he said. "Eventually, you start to go downhill, right?"

"As far as I know," she said. "But he's the oldest one of us. I'm going by what I was told by him."

"So, it could all be bullshit."

She smiled.

"I can see that, yes."

"Then what the hell are we supposed to do?" he said, rolling another smoke. "I've come up against a lot of different kinds of strange in this world. Some of it really good, like you, but then there's *this* shit."

Veronique gently slapped the smoke from his hand.

"I was wrong to suggest that we run," she said. "Whatever we're supposed to do, we do it *together*. Run or head right to him, we do it side by side."

He looked at her and his hard look softened.

"And Josephine?"

"Her too," she said, swallowing. "She's always going to be our baby, but we can't protect her if she's away from us."

"I reckon, you'll handle that?" he said.

"You too," she said smiling. "Just because your wife and daughter are different than you doesn't mean she shouldn't know how to shoot the pecker off of a turtle at a hundred feet."

Wall's eyebrows raised. This is what he had once told his daughter in private when showing her how to shoot a gun. Josephine turned out to be a dead shot.

"I know I wasn't supposed to hear that, Tom Wall. I just never said anything about until now. Fathers and daughters have a different relationship than mothers and daughters. It explains why her language is as *colorful* as it is," she said, chuckling.

Wall allowed a small smile.

"We need to figure this out," he said. "We need to decide how to meet him."

"On our terms," Veronique said finally. "*Only* on our terms."

Wall's eyes narrowed and look across the horizon.

"It's a start," he said.

***

Wall and Veronique went back in the house to get a few hours of sleep before planning on what to do. In the daffodils off to the side of the porch, there was a buzzing that no one was around to hear. There was a march of spiders that no one was awake to see. And no one was aware of what was beginning to form under the porch and in the daffodils.

CHAPTER 8

San Antonio Texas

Henry Robb was on the verge of crying as he led his horse through what was left of San Angelo. It wasn't all the burned out buildings, or the thick smoke that still poured from some of the larger buildings.

It was the bodies of the women and children strewn around town. Some were burned, some were broken, some looked partially devoured, but all were dead. It was the worst thing Robb had ever seen.

McCall had stayed in what was left of the post office to try and get the telegraph machine up and running, so he hadn't gotten to see the true state of the small town.

Robb hoped for his sake that he'd skip that part.

No one needed to see this.

Robb was looking for signs of survivors, but he was quickly realizing that this man Trask wasn't one to leave anyone alive. This was a bigger problem than anyone had thought.

He was just glad Trask wasn't there when they had arrived.

Robb turned his horse around and headed back towards the post office. There weren't any survivors. Just corpses and smoke.

**

McCall was surprised the telegraph was in relatively good condition. The litter of corpses were daunting though, and he threw up a few times moving the bodies out of the office. The three bodies in the office had been torn and mangled. One young lady had her head twisted nearly off. It hung on by a thick swatch of skin as the head lay unnaturally to one side; a look of sheer terror on her face.

There was a part of him that didn't want to believe that one man was capable of so much death and destruction. As he dragged the young lady out of the office, he was grateful they had missed Trask by twelve hours at least, but he also knew they'd catch up to him sooner than later.

And they'd need a hell of a lot more help to take him down.

He went back inside and grabbed a stool that hadn't been smashed. He sat in front of the telegraph and began to type a message to Corpus Christi. That sheriff needed to know what exactly was headed his way.

He wondered if Wall really had retired because they sure as hell could use an experienced hand.

***

Wall stepped into Clancy's office first thing in the morning to see his friend already up and about. This was unusual for Clancy as he had a tendency to sleep in on a regular basis. Corpus Christi had a somewhat easy reputation for being a pretty peaceful place and Clancy, good sheriff as he was, took a bit of advantage of that more often than not. Today, apparently, was not one of those days.

"Tommy, I'm glad you're here," Clancy said, sitting down behind his cluttered desk. "Saves me the trouble o' comin' to find you."

Wall frowned.

"I take it you weren't comin' for breakfast," Wall said, sitting down as well.

"Christ on his throne no," Clancy said. "Got a telegram from San Antonio, or what's left of it. Take a look."

He took the telegram and handed it to Wall who read it immediately.

THE WESTERN UNION TELEGRAPH COMPANY

TO: CAPT. TOMAS WALL (RET), SHERIFF OF
       CORPUS CRISTI

FROM: CPL. R. MCCALL

RE: FUGITIVE UPDATE. TRASK IS STILL HEADED
       YOUR WAY. 12 HOURS OR SO BEHIND AND
       GAINING. HE'S KILT ALL SAN ANTONIO AND
       BURNED MOST OF IT DOWN. APPROACH WITH
       CAUTION, SHOOT TO KILL. NEVER SEEN

```
THIS  BEFORE.  WOULD  APPRECIATE  HELP.
SENDING FOR MILITARY IN AUSTIN.
```

"They keep spellin' your name wrong," Clancy said. Wall shook his head.

"Ain't a spellin' bee, Clanc. Henry's a good man."

"Oh, I don't mean nothing. Just trying to stay light." Clancy said. "Because that telegram is goddamn terrifying."

"Sure is," Wall said, looking up from it. "Well, the good news is, I'm in. So's the missus."

"The missus? You can't put her or your little one in danger, Tom." Clancy said.

"Ain't your call anymore," Wall said. "I reckon you need to deputize who you can on this. Veronique was a sheriff and a pretty damn good one. Don't shoo away help on account she's a woman."

"I know, but it don't feel right." Clancy said.

"Well, it can feel wrong all you want, but she's in."

"I can always refuse her help, Tommy."

Wall smiled.

"She's one you don't have to deputize," Wall said, showing Clancy his Texas Ranger badge pinned to his vest. "I took care of that this morning on my end."

Clancy's face turned red.

"You know, that wouldn't hold up if I pushed it."

Wall laughed.

"If you want to tell her that, be my guest." Wall said standing up. "But I'd wait till after this is all done to do that. You ain't gonna want to piss her off when she's *already* pissed off."

"You're serious." Clancy said.

"You know me to make a lot of jokes?"

"Fair enough," Clancy said, sighing. "I'll go make some deputies. Plan?"

"Have 'em all meet me at Paul Brine's stable at noon. We got stuff to go over." He began to walk out of the office. He stopped and turned back. "No half asses, Clancy. This Trask is a seriously bad man."

"How bad?"

Wall looked at him, hard. For the first time, Clancy saw Wall's eyes how they had been described in those penny dreadfuls: cruel and deadly.

"Son of a bitch killed a whole town. Pretty fuckin' bad." Wall said and left the office.

***

"I heard you and Daddy talkin' last night," Josephine said, with a mouth full of bacon.

Veronique smiled and looked at her.

"You listen to us a lot," she said. "What did you hear?"

"Well, I heard Daddy say some bad words, mostly. Like he was mad, but not at you."

"Well, sometimes we do get mad at each other, and your father does have a colorful pallet when he speaks sometimes."

"But he doesn't get mad like that at you."

Veronique nodded.

"Nor I him." She said. "So, are you worried about something?"

Josephine grabbed another hunk of bacon and crammed it into her mouth.

"Not really," Josephine said. "But the spiders think there's something to worry about."

Veronique raised an eyebrow.

"The spiders you say?"

Josephine nodded.

"They don't talk to me a whole lot, but I know there's something going on. I hear them talking to each other."

"What are they saying?" Veronique said. This was worrisome somehow.

"They just keep saying that they have to be ready," Josephine said. "But don't say for what. It's just that over and over. It makes me sad because they used to talk to me."

"Do you know why they don't?"

The little girl shook her head.

"Makes me sad," Josephine said, looking at her plate.

Veronique put a hand on her daughter's hand and gave it a squeeze.

"Things happen for a reason, love. Maybe they're busy trying to do something..." She let her voice trail off because she had no idea what to say.

"I know," Josephine said. "They're always doing *something*,"

"Josephine, when did you know you could talk to the spiders?"

The little girl simply shrugged.

"I've always talked to them," she said. "They just started talking back to me one day. Why?"

"Well," Veronique began. "I didn't know they could talk. I guess I never tried talking to them."

Josephine looked down.

"Momma," she started. "There's some other stuff I can do too," She sounded ashamed.

"I know sweetheart."

Josephine looked up.

"You do?"

"We've watched you do all sorts of amazing things, Josephine. You're a very special girl."

"I'm strange," Josephine nearly whispered.

"So is your Momma," Veronique said, smiling.

"No, you're all pretty and proper." She replied. "I'm not any of that. There's stuff I can do, Momma. I don't know how or why, but I just do them."

"As I said darling, you're special." Veronique said. "And I'm going to tell you why. Right now."

***

Trask rode slowly, heading towards Corpus Christi. He knew he was being followed and that made him smile. He'd surprise them by *not* killing them. He'd damn sure disable them; he didn't need them trying to kill him, but he'd show them he wasn't without mercy.

Besides, he needed very much to explain the town he'd left behind.

He'd lost his composure and really, could anyone blame him? He'd been misunderstood, certainly for what he was and what he'd done in the past and the recent past was no exception. If he could only find a way to express that all of the violence and death wasn't who he was. Certainly, not who he was trying to be which was something of a hero.

He took in a deep breath. He liked the idea of being a hero very much. He just needed a *way* to be a hero. The idea that Bosen had put into his ear all those years ago about the town, eliminating the unsavory element...well, it was perfect. When he destroyed Bosen, he did it out of love for coming up with the idea in the first place. He regretted killing him later, of course. But there wasn't a reason why he couldn't attempt the same thing on his own.

Bosen had done it. How hard could it be?

He would find Viorica and her offspring. He'd kill the man, Wall. Then he would save them both. Wall had no idea how to be a hero, much less be a husband or father. He'd be doing them all a favor.

Especially Viorica.

As angry as he was, he wouldn't always be. He'd learn to get over it. He'd overcome so much, he could overcome anything.

And a new child! Why, he couldn't stay that angry around children. Admittedly, he was riding away from a town that now wore the burden of dead, burned children by his hand, but again, not his fault.

Bad timing.

Bad circumstances.

Misunderstandings...

It couldn't be him.

Could it?

There was a small sliver of doubt that always lurked in his head. The sliver was now finding a voice though, and that was distressing. Very distressing.

He couldn't make out what the voice was saying and it didn't say it all the time, but the buzzing was there. Always in the background.

He wasn't wrong, though. It wasn't his fault. It couldn't be his fault. You don't live for over two hundred years by being stupid or arrogant.

He would be a hero.

The buzzing became louder, but he ignored it.

He was *already* a hero.

He'd be able to tell that to the two men following him in a few hours. He'd make them understand. He'd send them ahead and maybe they'd prepare something for him.

He thought of a reception that might await him and this made him smile again.

***

Corpus Christi, Texas

"You know, a lot of these folks is gonna get themselves killed," Brine said.

Wall leaned against the opening of Brine's stables and said nothing. It was nearly noon and he was waiting for Clancy to assemble some folks to help with Trask. Brine wasn't wrong, Wall thought. But seeing as Trask just killed a whole damn town, he had to try to at least make it a fight.

"From what you say," Brine continued. "He's a lot more than just a killer. Goddamn lunatic."

"That's about right." Wall said. "But he ain't a *stupid* lunatic. He's something else."

"What exactly?" Brine asked. "Something like..."

Wall's eyes snapped to Brine.

"Like what?"

Brine smiled.

"You know who." He said. "I ain't blind or stupid which is why I ain't said nothin' about it til right now. Your missus. She's something else too, ain't she?"

Wall glared.

"I ain't sayin' nothin' bad about her. Just a point of fact."

"Is it?" Wall said.

Brine, who had been sitting, stood up.

"Yeah, it is. That being said, I care a lot about your girls and I don't wanna see nothin' bad happen to you or anyone here."

Wall nodded, but he held his glare.

"I ain't sayin' nothin' to nobody either. Ain't nobody else's business, Tom."

Wall's glare softened.

"I appreciate that, Pop. A hell of a lot." Wall said.

"You thank me when we take this son of bitch down," Brine said. "Where the hell is Clancy?"

Tom turned around and looked down the street. It was empty.

"Where the hell is anyone?" Brine spat.

"This ain't good," Wall said.

***

"We're going to try something because we're late. Are you up for it?"

Josephine looked at her mother suspiciously.

"What do you mean Momma?"

Veronique smiled.

"Well, you know how you can run really fast?"

Josephine nodded.

"We're going to do that. Right now, you and I."

"Okay!" she said. "Where are we going to run?"

Veronique squatted down to eye level and looked in Josephine's eyes.

"Mr. Brine's stable."

Josephine made a perfect "O" with her mouth.

"Momma, that's really far, can we do that?"

"We can do a *lot* of things, lovey. But before we do, you have to know a few things. After we're done, you're going to be very hungry. I'll bring you something to eat. Don't question what it is okay?"

"Is it a cookie?"

"No, it's not a cookie."

"What is it?"

"What did I just tell you?"

"That you'd give me something to eat."

"What else?"

Josephine shuffled her feet.

"Not to question it?"

"That's right."

"But what is it?"

"Hush now." Veronique said. "Are you ready?"

Josephine nodded.

"But how do we do it? I mean when I do it, it just happens."

"You need to picture where you want to go in your head and run there. Now, before you do-"

Before she could finish, Josephine smiled and vanished.

"So like your father," Veronique said and ran after her.

CHAPTER 9

Josephine had run fast before, but since she was running further than she had before, she noticed a few different things.

First, if you ran that fast while smiling, bugs would be sucked into your mouth and nose. This she learned in the first few seconds of the run. She made a yucky sound, and put her head down. Second, it was really windy. Her Momma had made her brush her hair before coming outside, but she could feel her hair flying all over the place. Momma would be mad.

Before she knew it, she was just outside of Mr. Brine's stable.

She looked around. She'd actually done it! She heard her father and Mr. Brine. She laughed and jumped in a little circle.

And then, like her Momma said, she realized she was hungry.

Really hungry.

Hungrier than she'd ever been.

She looked around, eyes wild, in agony. She'd never felt like this before and she wasn't as terrified as she was hungry.

She heard a sound coming from about twenty feet away. Her head darted in the direction and saw an old dog, lazing around, looking for somewhere to sit. She could hear flies buzzing around its head. She could see them clearly, and she could also see the bit of his ear that was bleeding.

The dog's ear flapped, swatting away the flies for a moment, then they were back.

Josephine could smell the blood and without thinking, she ran toward the dog.

***

"What in the goddamn hell is *that*?" Brine said.

A high pitched whine exploded from behind the stable. Wall looked at Brine and then ran out of the doorway, heading for the noise.

When Wall reached the back, there came another whine followed by a loud snap. He looked and looked away.

"No," he said and then ran towards his daughter who had already begun devouring the dog.

She had grabbed the dog and still running, taken him another twenty feet or so. She had snapped the dog's neck and was now biting and tearing chunks of the dog with her teeth. She was swallowing them whole. She did this again and again as Wall came closer. He felt his face getting hot. He wanted to yell to her, to tell her to stop, but he couldn't. There was a scream inside of him that he wanted to let out, but he knew it would scare his daughter.

He was ten feet away and he slowed down.

She had nearly finished eating the dog entirely.

She dropped the dog's back left leg and backed away from it. She looked around, scared and confused. She looked everywhere for something until her eyes saw Wall.

She stood, looking at him for a long time. He looked at her back. Her face was covered in blood and meat. She looked like she was going to cry and she began to shake.

Wall dropped to her knees and held his arms out to her. She ran into him, nearly knocking him over and cried hard into his chest. Wall wrapped his arms around her and didn't say a word.

He didn't have to say anything, because really, what could he possibly say to her?

Moments later, Veronique appeared right over them. She began to weep as well, but just stood there, watching the two people she loved most in the world.

Finally, Wall spoke.

"We should go clean you up darlin'," he said.

Josephine continued to cry.

"I'll take her," Veronique said. "I'll take care of her."

Josephine looked up and saw her mother. She held a hand out to her but refused to let Wall go.

Veronique took her hand and squeezed it.

"I..." was all Josephine could say.

"Shhhhh," her mother said. "Come with Momma."

She continued to hold Wall.

"Momma can help you more than I can, sweet pea." Wall said. "Why don't you go with her?"

"But, she'll know what I done," Josephine whispered.

"She already does," Wall said. "And it's okay. She ain't mad and neither am I."

"Come here, little one." Veronique said. "I'll take you back home."

Finally, Josephine relented. She let go of Wall and went to Veronique who swept her up. She hugged her daughter very tightly and was hugged back in kind.

Wall stood up, ribs aching a little.

"What are you going to do?" Veronique asked.

"Same plan, less people." Wall said. "Clancy done run off. It's just us."

Veronique nodded.

"You can't handle him alone." She said.

"I reckon there's only one way to find out." Wall said. "Besides, I ain't never alone. I'll be home soon. Get her out of here."

Wall kissed his wife and the back of Josephine's head.

"Love you." He said.

"We love you too," and she ran, vanishing almost instantly.

Wall watched as they blinked out of sight.

He heard Brine behind him.

"Sorry about your dog," Wall said.

Brine coughed and then laughed.

"Fuck that dog," he said. "We got bigger problems."

***

Trask stood with his arms and face up to the night sky. His eyes were wide open and he looked at the moon and stars. He felt gloriously small in the face of the universe.

And yet, so amazingly large on the face of the earth.

He was the lord of all he surveyed.

This made him smile.

He was God.

He'd toyed with that very idea for centuries; being God. He didn't think there was such of thing. He'd eliminated every reasonable theory about a higher being and at least, in this place looking at the night sky he knew without a doubt that he, in fact was God.

No one stood to oppose him. Things lived or died at his whim or his mercy. He was all powerful. He was supreme. He was all.

All he needed now, was his sire and her whelp.

With them gone, there would be only he.

And that was good and right as it needed to be.

But first things first.

He lowered his arms and regarded his two guests.

"Gentlemen," he said. "I have realized my purpose in this world. My place in it to be exact."

McCall and Robb stared at Trask with wild terrified looks. The two men had been crucified in front of a large fire. They weren't nailed, but tied to the handmade crosses Trask had made them build. They said nothing.

"I have come to realize that I am your God." Trask continued. "I just have to decide exactly what kind of God I shall be. Since you two have been following me for a while and have seen my handiwork up close, I am asking for your suggestions. I will need disciples after all."

McCall coughed and winced.

Trask looked at him, eyes wide with anticipation.

"Yes, brother? You wish to speak?"

McCall coughed some more, spitting blood.

"Let us go,' McCall said through spasms of coughing.

"No," Trask said, moving closer to him. "That isn't a suggestion I'm looking for,"

McCall blinked.

Trask walked to the base of the cross and looked up.

"Don't you cough on me," Trask warned.

"Please..."

"Please what?"

"Let us go,"

Trask punched McCall in his leg, breaking it. McCall screamed briefly before passing out. The bone in his lower leg cut through and stuck out of his pants. Robb remained still, breathing heavy.

"No," Trask said. "Maybe you aren't a worthy disciple. You then," His attention switched to Robb.

Robb looked ahead, lips moving.

"I can't hear you, brother."

"Kill..."

"Kill? Yes, I will do that, but I need to be just in it. Kill what?"

"Kill..." Robb said again, still looking forward.

Trask was growing impatient.

"Kill what?"

Robb coughed and cleared his throat.

"Kill me, bastard." Robb said finally.

Trask was furious.

"You have no vision," Trask said. "You have no respect! You and your stupid friend here had a chance to sit at my right hand! And you want death?"

He snarled at Robb, but Robb surprised him and spit directly into his face.

"I'll take death if it means I ain't gotta hear your goddamn *jawin'* anymore," Robb said through labored breathing.

Trask nearly exploded, but stood there with an angry surprised expression.

He had an idea.

"You loathe me, don't you?"

Robb said nothing, waiting for his end.

"Well," Trask said, wiping his face and then licking his hand. "I think I have a much better idea."

Trask lifted up Robb's pant leg and bit into it. Robb gritted his teeth and groaned at the pain as Trask drank from the wound.

***

Veronique took Josephine and lay her down in her room. She began to undress the little girl who was still awake, and shaking from fear. Veronique sang a little song to her-one that she sang when Josephine was afraid of storms. She peeled off the bloody clothes and wadded them up in a pile. She then picked up the little girl and took her to the little river than ran behind their house. She got in the river with her and washed her carefully. The water was cold, but Josephine didn't react to it.

She sang the entire time until the little girl was clean. She then carried her back to the house, lay her down again, this time on hers and Wall's bed. She took off her own clothes that by now were wet and stained with blood. She quickly dressed in something practical' a part of Wall's pants and one of his shirts.

She picked out more flexible clothes for Josephine from the little girl's room. A small pair of dungarees, a button down shirt and a small pair of boots.

She dressed the little girl who still shook and looked at her mother, bleary eyed.

"Josephine," Veronique said. "I'm going to explain to you what happened. I know you're scared by it, but you didn't do a single thing wrong, except to go ahead without me."

Josephine said nothing.

"You're a little girl. You are partly made from your Daddy and partly from me. Daddy is a man. A good decent man. The best I've ever known. And you're partly me."

Josephine looked into space, crying slightly.

"I used to be a little girl just like you. Part of that little girl is in you too. But, I was changed when I wasn't too much older than you I was made into..."

Veronique struggled to find the right word for what she had become.

"Something different." She decided. "You look like a little girl and you *are* a little girl, but you're something else too. What happened today is part of that. You're different and it doesn't always have to happen like it did today. I'm going to teach you how to control it. To use it. To hide it when you need to. And most importantly, to know that it isn't your fault."

Josephine blinked at her.

"Monsters," Josephine said.

"I try not to think that's what we are," Veronique said. "I've met worse people who were just regular normal folks."

"I ate a *dog*," Josephine said.

"Yes. Yes you did. And you know what, you're going to eat *more*. Cows, horses whatever you can find because you will try *not* to eat people."

Josephine's eyes went wide.

"I would never!"

"You might not have a choice one day," Veronique said sadly.

"Have you?"

Veronique closed her eyes.

"More than my share,"

"Were they bad people?"

"Not all of them," Veronique said, tearing up.

Josephine looked shocked.

"Why?"

Veronique looked at her daughter and wiped a tear away.

"There's a man...an actual monster who is coming for us. You, your father and I. He's the one who made me into what we are."

Veronique was now openly crying.

"Why didn't Daddy take care of him?" Josephine asked. "Daddy could take care of that man."

"Daddy's going to try," Veronique said. "But as good as Daddy is, as tough as he is, this monster might be too much for him."

Josephine frowned.

"I don't believe that for a minute." The little girl said. "Nobody's tougher than Daddy. Or you."

"This monster might be."

The mention that someone might be better at something than her parents lit a fire in the little girl.

"Tell me what happened when you were a little girl, Momma."

Veronique relayed the story as honestly as she could. She spoke for a half hour without stopping. Josephine gasped a few times and cried at the end. Veronique relayed the story of how she and Wall met and their adventures before deciding to stop when she became pregnant.

"I know that is a lot to tell a girl your age," Veronique said. "And I know you might not understand all of it, but that is the truth. That's where we are."

Josephine sat, with tears still in her eyes. She hugged her mother tightly and her mother returned the hug in kind.

"Momma?"

"Yes love?"

"I'm gonna need a minute."

Veronique pulled away.

"A minute for what?"

Josephine said nothing.

Veronique tried to smile.

"I'll give you some time to yourself. And then we have to go."

Josephine nodded and hopped off of her parent's bed. She walked through the house to the outside porch.

Veronique sat and sobbed, hoping she had done the right thing.

***

"Hello?" Josephine said to the spiders that lived in the daffodils. "You need to talk to me."

The spiders who had all be still and waiting for something to wander into their webs turned in her direction. There were five of them today where there used to be more.

"You will talk to me today. Please?"

The largest spider of the five left the web and crawled up to the post on the porch.

It simply stood there.

"You can understand me and I can understand you." Josephine said. "Is it because of what I am?"

The spider walked in a small circle and then spoke.

"Not exactly, but it is part of it," the spider said. "You listen, which is what no one else does. But we can understand what you say because of what you are. We cannot talk to your mother in this way."

"Why not?"

"Because she will not listen. She is too old."

"Oh," Josephine said, although she didn't really understand. "There is a bad man coming. He is like me and my Momma."

"We know this." The spider said.

"How?"

"We just know. We are all connected. He is one of you but he is an old one of you. He is not good."

"Okay. What can we do?"

"You should kill him," the spider said. "That is what you should do."

"How?"

"You say *how* a lot," the spider said. "You know how."

"No, I *don't*. And neither does my Momma and she would know how, but she don't."

"When the time comes you will know how." The spider said. "It is in you to do this. If you were older, we wouldn't be able to help you."

"But, you're not helping me. I don't know how to do *anything*!"

"You know more than you think you do," the spider said. "So does your mother. You tell her that."

"What about my Daddy?"

The spider began speaking rapidly and almost incoherently.

"Slow down!" Josephine said. "You ain't makin' sense."

"We do not care for your father," said the spider. "He steps on us. We do not care what happens to him."

"He's my Daddy and I told him to stop squashing you." Josephine said. "What can he do to help?"

The spider said nothing.

"Can you just tell me what I can do?" Josephine asked.

"I have said enough," the spider replied. "If I think of anything I will let you know. Until then, you need to feed. Much more than today. You and your Momma."

And with that, the spider walked back to the daffodils without another word.

Josephine thought about this for a moment and went back into the house. She would need to see about getting her and her Momma fed.

Something was coming.

CHAPTER 10

Robb was coming to, and he realized it was daylight. His vision was blurry. He also found that he wasn't on the cross anymore. Maybe, it was a nightmare and he was just now waking up. He blinked a few times and his eyes cleared up. He was on the dusty ground. He saw a spider walking near his face and he sat up to get away from it.

He looked at his hands and wrists. There weren't any rope marks although they still felt a little sore. He squeezed his hands and they felt okay, just a dull ache that went all the way up his arms.

But, there was dried blood on them.

He grabbed some dirt from the ground and rubbed them between his hands to get the blood off and it worked a little bit.

McCall.

Where the hell was he?

He stood up carefully and looked around.

To his horror, there were two crosses still in the ground, but the one McCall had been on had been snapped in half. The top part was still burning in the fire from the night before. But, there wasn't any sign of McCall.

Except, there was.

There was his boots for one thing.

One boot, his left one it looked like. There was a gnarled white bone sticking out of it and some skin hanging over the side.

He looked closer and there were bits of unburned clothes still smoking in the fire.

Robb looked down on himself and saw that his shirt and pants were torn; shredded but, covered in dried blood and meat. He tore at them in a panic. He started to yell and scream.

"Yell all you want," Trask said behind him. "That won't bring anyone, brother."

Robb whirled around and saw Trask standing, with his arms behind his back.

"Welcome back," Trask said. "You have a good night's sleep?"

Robb stepped backward, still clawing at his clothes.

"Easy now," Trask said. "You've had a hard journey."

"What the hell happened?" Robb said.

"You're a disciple now," Trask said. "You are an example of my mercy."

"Where's McCall?"

"In your belly," Trask said. "But you already knew that, didn't you?"

Robb gagged.

"Don't you retch now, brother."

Robb gagged and fought the urge.

"You're one of my kind now. We are on the same side. Isn't that better?"

Robb dropped to his knees.

"Why...why..."

"You need to calm down, now. Can't have you losing your mind, young man."

Robb's mind was a swirling mess. Bits and flashed of the night before came and went at a maddening pace. He remembered being bitten. Then being ripped off the cross. Then...drinking blood from Trask. He fought the urge to spill his guts yet again.

Then he remembered McCall screaming.

He remembered eating his longtime friend and partner. He remembered McCall screaming, passing out, coming to again and passing out again and again as Robb ate him whole. He remembered breaking the cross off at the center when he could no longer reach him to eat. He slammed the cross down and went on eating and eating.

He remembered changing. His limbs grew out. His clothes could not contain the growth and tore, but not completely off. He remembered tearing off huge strips of meat from McCall as he mewled and cried. He remembered looking into McCall's eyes before...

Robb let out a loud cry and let it roar to the bright Texas morning sky.

Trask brought his hands from behind his back. In one hand, he held aloft McCall's torn off head.

"If you're through," he said calmly. "We can have breakfast and discuss what comes next."

***

SPIDERS IN THE DAFFODILS

Corpus Christi, Texas

Wall rode back to the house slowly. It had all been for nothing. Pop and he talked in circles while no one at all showed up for the defense plan. That goddamn sheriff Clancy had run off and now, his daughter had nearly lost her mind. He couldn't think of a single thing to do.

He thought of how bad it was when he and Veronique were on the run. They had no idea how easy they'd had it. When they stopped running, they became domesticated. That was the one thing Wall had never truly wanted because of things like this Trask fellow.

Trask.

He never feared things that were right in front of him and he hadn't ever planned on that happening to him. Yet, here it was. If Trask was right in front of him, he'd at least be able to try something. *Anything.* As it was, he'd have to wait from him to get to Corpus Christi in his own sweet ass time and Wall hated that.

He needed to see Josephine and talk with Veronique to see what kind of weaknesses he could exploit.

He kicked the horse a little bit to hurry him along.

He wanted to see his girls.

Wall knew there was a really good chance he wasn't walking away from this one.

***

Dinero, Texas

Trask and Robb rode into the small town of Dinero. They had to share a horse as both Trask and Robb had eaten the other two horses, but Trask didn't mind sharing the ride. He wasn't alone anymore. He had a brother. A disciple. Even maybe a friend.

He wasn't too sure about the friend part, as Robb would often burst into tears at the drop of a hat, but he was quieter now at least.

He needed somewhere to get his companion new clothes and maybe even a few drinks. Perhaps an evening of some fun to let off some steam would loosen up his new counterpart.

It certainly couldn't hurt.

Trask had vowed out loud that he wouldn't kill anyone in this little town unless provoked. They were simply stopping off before reaching their destination which from Trask's estimations, was only about fifty or so miles away.

He found a hotel and tied up the horse. He told Robb to stay put and to not attract attention to himself. Robb looked at him blankly but nodded.

Trask walked into the small lobby and headed for the front desk. A small pudgy man in an ill-fitting suit looked at him and smiled.

"Howdy!" the man said. "Name's Clive. Get you a room?"

Trask smiled back.

"Yes. For two please. And is there a back entrance? My travelling companion is in a bit of a state."

"Sure thing. I'll put you folks on the top floor. Round the back, there's stairs leading up to it. How long you reckon you'll be here?"

"Just over night," Trask said. "Does this town have a tailor?"

Clive thought a moment.

"Well, I can get the undertaker. He's the closest thing to one here."

"Appropriate," Trask said. "Please send for him at once."

Trask took out a wad of money and laid it on the counter. Clive's eyes went wide.

"This should cover it all. Key please?"

"Why, yes sir!" Clive said, grabbing a key from behind the counter. "Hell, that's enough for a few days at least."

"Consider the rest a tip," Trask said, walking back out of the hotel lobby. "Also, fetch a bath if you have one. Let me know when your man arrives."

Clive was nearly beside himself at his fortune.

"Billy!" he called out. A scrawny boy came running from upstairs.

"Yes Poppa?" the boy said.

"Go get Mr. Davies. Tell him to bring some clothes here on the double."

"Clothes?" The boy looked confused.

"Just go do it, goddamn you!" Clive said. "Tell him it's a paying customer who is still alive. I got to get a bath together."

The boy shrugged and ran out of the door. As he rounded the front steps, he saw a man in black leading another man by his arm around to the back of the building.

"That can't be good," the boy said running.

***

Trask led Robb up the stairs and into the small room. There was only one bed and Trask sighed. For now, it would do. He pushed Robb onto the bed.

"You relax, my friend." Trask said. "I'll get you cleaned up and dressed properly. You and I have a very big day tomorrow."

Robb looked up at the ceiling and blinked.

"Just relax," Trask repeated. "A good bath and a suit of new clothes will bring you around." He smiled. He was a good friend.

Trask walked out onto the stair case that he had just climbed. He looked out and thought about the look on Viorica's face when he found her. He thought maybe he'd kill her slowly. Maybe, he'd let his new friend kill the whelp. Or maybe...maybe he'd make Viorica kill her own husband and then kill her.

There were so many options. He tried to stamp the thoughts down because he knew, they'd never live up to how he would build them. He decided he'd see what would happen when he got there.

He couldn't wait.

***

The smell was the first thing that hit Wall when he walked into the house. He knew it. That goddamn jelly. It was hot and sweet smelling, but it smelled like rotten apples. He damn near gagged as he walked into the kitchen. There he saw Veronique and Josephine jarring the foul smelling stuff into large jars. They were both wearing handkerchiefs over their faces and thick work gloves.

"What in the hell are you two doing?" he said, gagging.

"Daddy!" Josephine said, running to him. She hugged him tightly around his waist.

"Hi baby," he said. "You okay?"

"I'm good Daddy, real good."

"Hello, lover." Veronique said, pouring more of the jelly into a jar. "I'll hug you in a moment."

Wall looked confused and just a little nauseated.

"Darlin', I appreciate you occupyin' the girl with something to do but, Jesus jumped up baldheaded, why *this*?"

She looked at him and although he could only see her eyes, he knew she was smiling.

"I don't like it either, but it's going to come in handy."

"I reckon you'll explain?"

"Yes love. Why don't you take Josephine onto the porch with you."

"Gladly," he said, picking his daughter up and walked out of the room.

On the porch, Josephine took off her handkerchief and smiled at Wall.

"Smells bad, don't it Daddy?"

"Hell yes it does," Wall said, sitting down with her on his lap. "You didn't eat any did you?"

"Nope," she said.

"Good. Don't. 'Bout the worst thing I ever put in my mouth." He said, smiling a little. "Don't quite get why your Momma is makin' it though."

"It was my idea," Josephine said. "Me and Momma, we're allergic to it."

"Well, goddamn, I guess so am I." he said.

"No, you just don't *like* it." Josephine said. "This stuff can *kill* me and Momma."

Wall opened his mouth to speak and then closed it.

"What?"

"Yes sir," she said. "Momma told me about the last time she made this stuff. Said she got awful sick."

"Well, that wasn't on account of..."

"Yes it was," Veronique said, walking out onto the porch. "Deathly sick if you remember. When we first moved here."

Wall nodded.

"From the berries?" he said.

"The whole tree," she said, sitting next to Wall. "It's a variation of a tree near where I lived in Slovenia. It's called a Hawthorn."

"So, you're allergic to this tree? Why didn't you let me cut it down?"

"You aren't understanding me," she said. "It can kill me. It can kill Josephine. And, it can kill *Trask*."

Wall stared at her then at Josephine who was giggling.

He frowned.

"So, we're gonna make him eat some toast with that jelly?" he said.

Veronique and Josephine laughed.

"If we hit him with it, it'll burn his skin." Veronique said. "It's a *weapon*, Tom."

Tom rubbed his chin.

"What about the rest of the tree?" he asked. "Because I have an idea of my own, now that this is sinkin' in."

***

Robb was trying to forget. Forget his name, the events of the past few days, simply everything. And he was failing miserably. He was doomed and he knew it.

He'd gotten bath and had managed to wash himself if only to prevent that bastard Trask from touching him anymore than he'd already done. He got measured and then fit with new clothes. The tailor / undertaker had brought a variety of suits and modified them on the spot. Nice man and he was still surprised that Trash had not only let him go, but had paid him as well.

To be fair, Robb had begun to feel better, but only because he thought it would be in his best interests to do so. He didn't know if he was dead or alive, but he could still feel pain. Still fear things and until he had a better grip of his surroundings, he thought it better to go along with whatever Trask asked of him.

But still, he tried to forget. Especially McCall.

He'd eaten his partner. There wasn't any coming back from that, no doubt. He pushed it to the Back of his mind over and over but it still kept coming back. The screams, the begging, all of it.

His best shot now was to see where this was all playing out. Trask had said they were going to Corpus Christi and Robb would go there too, but then he'd have to figure out what if anything he could do about it.

Trask kept telling Robb about what he wanted to happen and how much of a help he was going to be. Robb wasn't sure he wanted to be help at all. He'd have to sort that out on the way and ultimately when they got there.

Trask had mentioned Tom Wall in passing and that worried Robb. If there was one person who'd bring about his end, it would be Wall. He wasn't one of the most famous Texas Rangers for nothing He doubted Wall had ever come up against something like Trask (*or now himself)* but if there was a person who could possibly handle it, it would be Captain Tom Wall.

He hoped.

***

The entire Wall family went to bed late and Josephine had passed out almost as soon as she hit the pillow.

Wall and Veronique went to their bed as well, but didn't sleep right away.

Wall kissed Veronique hungrily as she kissed him. They clawed at their clothes while still standing up. Veronique tore off Wall's shirt with one hand as he tore open her shirt and grabbed her breasts. She ran her hands down his chest and found his belt, which she snapped in two. She pulled the pants down and grabbed his manhood. He moved from her breasts and wrapped his arms around her body, grabbing her ass. She moaned still kissing. She moved backwards, falling onto the bed with him on top of her. She spread her legs and took him inside of her. She wrapped her legs around him and pulled him in deeper. His hands stayed, grabbing her ass, lifting her up slightly as he slid in and out of her slowly at first, then fasted and faster.

They bucked against each other, almost never parting mouths or loins. Their friction reached a fever pitch and their kiss was broken when Veronique threw her head back and gasped. She dug her fingers into his back and he hissed in blissful agony. He rolled her on top of him and she rode him hard, her hips undulating back and forth as he rose to meet each thrust with his own. Sweat was pouring off of them both. She put both of her hands on his chest and again, her fingers dug in but never breaking the skin.

They made long, desperate love like that three more times that night, knowing full well that it may be their last. They savored every moment with each other, the way they always had done before.

Before dawn, they both fell asleep in each other's arms.

CHAPTER 11

Josephine could not sleep. She was scared, but she was excited too. She had spent most of the day being scared and she was still a little scared, but after talking to her mother, she felt better and she was going to be able to help.

She couldn't sleep and really didn't want to, but she kept trying. She closed her eyes and started to count backwards from fifty. This usually worked, but for some reason she'd done it four times and was still awake.

"Little girl," said a voice in the center of her brain. She knew the voice at once.

"Pajkov!" Josephine said. "I've missed you. Where have you been?"

"I've missed you too, little one." The spider said. "I've been looking out for you and I've come to warn you."

Josephine frowned.

"Warn me about what?"

"The monster coming for you and your family." Pajkov said. "He's dangerous. Very dangerous. More dangerous than your mother thinks. And getting closer."

"There's only one of him."

"He's the most powerful of your kind." Pajkov said. "He's hundreds of years old and he will not die easily."

"But he will die," Josephine said.

"Yes, he will. Eventually. But be careful."

"I will," Josephine said.

"I will help where I can," Pajkov said.

"How will you help?"

"You'll know." The spider said. "I'm going to go. You should sleep, little one."

"But I can't sleep."

"You will,"

Josephine yawned.

"I'll try," the little girl said.

And with that, the spider left.

Josephine fell fast asleep.

***

Trask and Robb rode towards Corpus Christi at a steady pace. Robb, with his own horse, was feeling much better, but still not fully well. He was wrestling with what he had become and what it had taken for him to be whatever the hell it was he had become.

The one thing now he wanted more than anything though, was for Trask to shut his mouth.

Trask insisted that they leave before the first light and had not stopped talking since. They ate the hotel manager and his boy before leaving so they would be ready for what they were about to do.

Or, what Trask had wanted them to do.

Robb was still not too sure of the plan or if there even was one. At one point, Robb simply decided to nod and say "yes" when he was expected to and just rode in silence.

Silence that was filled with the voice of Trask.

"The possibilities are endless," Trask said. "We kill the bitch and her whelp, and of course the Ranger. Then maybe, we convert the town. Maybe just half. I mean, the first half will need something to eat."

On and on, he talked and more and more Robb began to hate this thing riding next to him. Robb had always been a tolerant man and now he reckoned he was being a tolerant thing. But, his tolerance was fading quickly as his body kept changing.

He had to admit, the power he felt was incredible. He may have become something detestable, but he was powerful. His eyesight, always a little bad had improved greatly. He could see for miles upon miles. He could smell things miles away as well. He was strong too. He felt truly alive. His skin tingled in the Texas morning sun.

He found that he could lose himself simply looking in the distance, listening to all the things he was riding towards, until of course, Trask opened his mouth.

"To be a true God," Trask continued. "Is to know true peace. Don't you feel peaceful, brother?"

"Yup," Robb said automatically. "I surely do."

"Good!" Trask said, then asked an odd question. "So, why haven't you thanked me yet?"

Robb heard this and swallowed.

"What?"

"I said why haven't you said a thank you. I could have just eaten you or killed you and left you for the critters. Are you that ungrateful?"

Robb had to think about his answer.

"Well," he said. "I figured, I'd wait until we got all the way to Corpus Christi. I'm still settling into this skin. But, I expect I am grateful, so thanks."

Trask nodded.

"You're a very quiet man," Trask said. "I'm sorry if I came off as rude. Just been a long time since I had a riding companion."

"Nothin' to apologize for," Robb said. "When I rode with McCall, we would go thirty miles sometimes without sayin' a word. Just something that happens on the trail I guess."

Again, Trask nodded.

"I've been doing a lot of talking haven't I?"

"Yes sir," Robb said. "But I reckon that's cos you're excited."

Trask smiled.

"You can say that again!" he said, mood elevated. Trask began to talk again, almost nonstop for the next few hours as they came closer to Corpus Christi.

Robb began to consider what he was going to do when they got there. None of the options were good ones, even if he did nothing at all. He knew one thing though; he couldn't abide the killing of a woman or a child. He didn't even consider trying to kill Wall. But, he also couldn't imagine killing Trask either. Not that he didn't want to, but because he was too much for him to handle.

Robb tried not to sigh and kept riding.

***

Wall took the bullets out of the jar of jelly from the night before. They were sticky and he hoped that they wouldn't gum up the guns. This was a big risk he'd come up with and one he hoped worked.

He set them all up to dry. Then he'd have to wipe them down so they'd sit in the chamber and hope they shot. He had also cut off a lot of the wood which now sat in a pile in his stable. He didn't know when the hell Trask would show up, but he needed to be ready and he was afraid he was already going to be too late.

Veronique was still in bed, sleeping quietly. He had no doubt she'd be pissed that he let her sleep, but hopefully it was something she'd be able to get over if they lived through what was coming.

He was wiping bullets when he heard the door creak open.

Josephine walked in with something in her hand.

"Hi Daddy," she said.

"Hi sugarplum," he said, smiling.

"I had me an idea,"

"Let's hear it."

Josephine knew she was lucky in that whatever she had to say, even if it was silly, her Daddy always listened to it. And he always was honest with his thoughts on it, even if it was what he considered a bad idea.

"I dug this out of my dresser and thought it might be a better idea for me." She showed him her sling shot.

Wall couldn't help but smile.

"Well, that's not a bad idea, but you'd have to be closer to this feller than I'd like you to be." He said. "I thought you was looking forward to using the rifle."

"Oh, I am," she said. "But I'm a better shot with this,"

Wall nodded because it was true.

In teaching Josephine how to shoot, she turned out to be deadly accurate. However, he'd seen her do some amazing things with her sling shot. The trouble was, the sling shot was unreliable when the distance was too long. And Wall didn't want his little girl anywhere near Trask when he showed up.

"Let me show you something." She said.

She took a stone out of her pocket.

"Promise you won't get mad," she said.

"I can't promise I won't get mad, but I'll do my best." Wall said. "If you hit me with that, I'll be plenty mad."

"No, I won't. Watch this."

She took her sling shot, loaded it with the rock and aimed it up.

Wall didn't have time to think as she pulled the slingshot back and let the rock fly.

The rock shot out, hit the wooden roof and punched a hole through it. Wall's jaw dropped. A moment later there was a loud squawk and something fell onto the roof roughly. Wall ran outside to see what it was.

He looked up and saw a vulture strewn out dead on the roof. He looked up higher and saw three more vultures way high in the sky, circling.

Josephine walked out of the barn with her slingshot at her side.

"Are you mad because I shot through your roof?" she asked.

Wall laughed.

"Not as mad as this here vulture must've been," he said. "How'd you hit him without even seeing him?"

Josephine shrugged.

"I heard him," she said. She shuffled her feet. "I think."

"Well, damn, darlin'," Wall said. "I reckon you can use your sling shot."

Josephine beamed.

"But I still can use the rifle?"

"Hell yes, but bring that with you. You got a spare one of those?"

The girl shook her head.

"Well, maybe I'll give you mine," he said.

"You have a slingshot?" she asked.

Wall smiled.

"Course I do. There ain't a Texas Ranger worth a damn who ain't got one," he said.

"That's what we are," Josephine said. "Texas Rangers."

Wall smiled.

"I thought you was your Momma's deputy."

"I reckon I can be both," Josephine said and ran towards the house.

Wall had to laugh. Laughs were gonna be hard to come by sooner than later.

***

It was about noon when Robb noticed a rider heading right for them. He saw the man clearly. He was fat, red faced. He could smell whisky on him too.

"You see that?" Trask asked.

"Yup," Robb said.

"That Wall?"

"No sir," Rodd said. "Ain't got no idea who that is. He's about an hour away at this pace."

"Perhaps we should ride out and see who it is." Trask said. "What do you say?"

Robb for the first time in a long day and a half felt an older instinct kick in and he set spurs to use, lurching his horse ahead quickly.

Trask gave a laugh and did the same.

***

"I must be out of my goddamned mind," Clancy said out loud. "I mean, for Christ's sake,"

He had left the town yesterday before the meeting to head off what was coming to his town. He didn't want anyone else to get killed. If anything, he'd die keeping this dangerous bastard out of his town. If he could find him, of course and if he could convince him that what he was looking for wasn't there.

Clancy had always been a god awful shot. It had less to do with how much he drank and more to do with his terrible eyesight.

But, he could talk. He was not only good at it, he was a master bullshit artist. One of the drunks he'd put in his cage had told him he could sell people things that they'd already owned. This was true, Clancy had to admit. The man he'd thrown into jail was a man he'd spent five hours drinking with and just couldn't hold his liquor well at all.

Clancy's heart nearly stopped when he saw two riders, and then relaxed. He was looking for one man, and here were two. For all he knew, it was those two Rangers. Maybe, he could convince them to help him with his plan. Hell, if he couldn't talk at least one of them into it, he was really a horrible sheriff.

It wasn't that Clancy was afraid. He'd never been afraid of anything. His father beat him and his two brothers growing up until Clancy grew up bigger than anyone in the whole damn family. By age twelve, he'd beaten his father nearly to death with a plow hitch. His father never laid another hand on him again.

He rode harder, wanting to get this meeting under way. He relaxed a little. It looked like the two riders were riding to meet up with him as well. He reached down to his flask and took a deep pull. Maybe this would go better than he was hoping.

***

Trask and Robb slowed down when they saw Clancy more clearly. Clancy did the same and trotted over.

"How do you gents do this fine day?" Clancy said smiling.

"We're just fine sir," Trask said. "And you?"

"Oh ya know, not too awful," Clancy said. "I was wondering if you could help an old sheriff out with something."

"Ask away, constable." Trask said.

"Constable!" Clancy said beaming. "Now, right there makes you nearly kin. I've been trying to get my town to call me that to no avail. From Ireland you see,'

"I thought I detected the Emerald accent!" Trask said. "What a fine country. Great whisky and ladies as well."

Clancy laughed and slapped his knee.

"Oh lad, you just made me day." Clancy said.

He looked at the other man, who sat quietly on his horse. He noticed his badge which shown brightly in the sun.

"You Texas Rangers?" Clancy asked.

"Corporal Robb," Robb said. "How you doing sheriff?"

"Then that must mean you're McCall," Clancy said, looking back at Trask. "This must be the luckiest day ever for me."

"It just might be," Trask said.

"I got your telegram lads," Clancy said. "I was riding out hoping to catch this vile bastard before he gets to my town. One of my citizens is an old friend of yours I believe, Tom Wall."

Trask looked at Robb.

"Telegram you say," Trask said.

"Yeah, for sure. Said this bastard Trask, I believe, killed an *entire town*. Women and children and such. Awful business."

"And you were riding out to intercept him?" Trask asked. "All by your lonesome?"

Clancy laughed.

"Well with you fellas here, I guess that's make three of us don't it?"

Trask laughed as well.

"One would think," Trask said. "Tell, me constable, what plan do you have once you run into this bad man?"

"Well," Clancy began. "I was going to try and appeal to his humanity, ya know? Killin' women and children is no way to be. Not something a man does, is it?"

"Interesting," Trask said. "But if he's done this more than once, don't you think you'd better go in, with purpose?"

"You're probably right, of course. But truth is, I couldn't hit the side of a feckin' barn with a shotgun if it were right in front of me." Clancy said, laughing. Trask laughed as well.

"So still, you came out here looking for him anyway?" Trask asked. "I mean, that takes a lot of guts. And by yourself no less. Don't you think that takes a lot of guts, corporal?"

Robb nodded. He was starting to worry. This poor bastard had no idea what was right in front of him.

"Well, I have good news for you, constable." Trask said looking at Robb. "Corporal Robb and I caught that vile son of a bitch and strung him up just two nights ago."

Clancy's face turned red.

"You don't say?"

"Oh, I surely do." Trask said, trying not to laugh. "Your act of sheer bravery was for the naught. But, your town should know what you set out to do."

Clancy was nearly overjoyed at this news until he noticed something about McCall.

Something he couldn't quite place.

"Well, I appreciate the hell out of that," Clancy said. "Now then, what did you do with the body?"

"What?"

"Where's the body?" Clancy said. "Surely you've dropped it off somewhere. A night's rest and clean pressed suits. A right celebration you two had I'm sure, but...I'd feel better seeing his lowly corpse if it's all the same."

A small frown formed on Trask's face.

"That's not really protocol for a Texas Ranger, sheriff."

Clancy's heart sunk just as quickly as it had risen.

"Well, corporal McCall," Clancy said, hand going toward his gun. "I'd also like to see your badge."

"Lost it in the scuffle," Trask said.

"Is that a fact too?" Clancy said.

"Is there a problem?" Trask asked.

Clancy drew his gun and fired. Trask, who could have moved, didn't. He sat there still, calming his jittery horse.

Clancy had missed by a mile. Trask reached out and took the gun out of Clancy's hand.

"You really are a bad shot, aren't you constable?"

"I am," Clancy said "But I can spot bullshit really well."

Trask laughed.

"Whatever am I going to do with you," he said, beginning to growl.

"And what about you then?" Clancy said, pointing to Robb. "You're a phony Ranger as well?"

Robb pulled his gun and aimed it at Clancy.

"No sir, I am a Ranger," Robb said. "I just ain't practicing that particular occupation at the moment."

He fired three shots directly into Clancy's face.

Trask whirled to look at Robb.

"You killed him without permission," Trask snarled.

"I need your permission to shoot someone?"

Clancy's body slid off of the horse and landed with a sick thud.

"After the past two days, I thought that was something that you'd be aware of having to do," Trask said through his teeth.

"He was onto us," Robb said, holstering his gun. "I didn't see no reason to keep him alive."

"We could have sent him back to the goddamn town to spread the news that I was dead. And then ride in and kill everyone in sight."

Robb looked at him.

"We're gonna do that anyway," Robb said. "Why prolong it?"

Why couldn't Robb *understand* this? He was trying to calm himself down.

"Never mind," Trask said. "Let's ride already."

Robb looked at him.

"Hey, if you want me to ask if it's okay to kill someone, I got no problem with that. Unless I'm told otherwise, I usually go on what I know. Sorry if that's a problem."

Trask looked at him for a moment, then broke out into a grin.

"You know brother," he said. "The best part about being a teacher is that you can still learn something. And you sir, have taught me something important."

Robb looked at him blankly.

"I will learn to trust your instincts," Trask said. "You've been surviving as a mere man in this world by your instincts. It was a good thing I didn't kill you."

Robb nodded, not quite sure what he meant.

"Let's ride and get to work," Trask said.

The two men rode off, leaving the body of Clancy with his rather confused horse to the vultures.

***

Veronique lay in bed, looking up at the ceiling. She thought about the last time she saw Trask. She shuddered just thinking of him, but she was going to do more than think about him today.

She was going to kill him.

She had to.

If she didn't have Tom or Josephine, she would have run after him. Recklessly, of course. That's how she did everything back then, when she was just a monster.

Monster.

She'd spent so much time believing that that even now, she had a problem thinking otherwise.

But now she was a wife.

She was a mother.

She was above all else, a woman.

And she was loved.

That made the difference. For as much as he said he loved her, Trask only loved himself. When she rejected his advances, he'd grown angry. When he took her forcefully, he never took all of her. Just her body. Again and again, he did this, but he never had her.

She was Tom's now. She would always be his and he would always be hers.

And she would rather die than let Trask come between them.

That might just happen, she thought.

She couldn't let anything happen to him or to Josephine. The urge for her to go after Trask was overwhelming, but she resisted it. Tom had a plan and it was a good one, although untested. She hated that her little girl would be helping, but they had no choice. It was the whole family's fight now.

As responsible as she felt, she knew it was the right plan. Wall's instincts on things were very seldom wrong. She had to trust him on this one. He'd never let her down before and she didn't think he was about to start.

There were a lot of unknowns coming their way.

She got up and got dressed. Again, she dressed in Tom's clothes as they were practical for the day to come. She strapped on her guns and put her work gloves on as well. If that jelly she'd made got on her skin she'd burn for sure.

She looked at herself in the mirror.

She still looked to be in her late twenties even though she was much older. She wondered if they all lived through this, if she'd have to watch Tom die an old man.

She couldn't bear the thought of this and pushed the image aside.

That was a very long way off, she hoped. She pushed open the bedroom door and looked back at the bed. She smiled.

She hoped that there were so many more days ahead with her husband and her daughter.

***

Josephine leaned over the railing of the porch and looked at the daffodils.

"Y'all better hide and take cover," she said to the spiders. There were six spiders today.

One of the spiders turned.

"He's coming," the spider said. "We know. We knew before you did."

Josephine frowned.

"Well, you don't need to be rude about it," she said.

"We'll be ready," the spider said.

"What do you mean?"

"Go hide," the spider said.

This made Josephine mad.

"Well, if my Daddy could hear you he'd squash you for sure for being so damn *rude*," she said and went to climb the roof.

The spiders said nothing.

***

Wall finished his task in the barn and looked at it carefully. He'd never built anything like this and hoped it would work. He heard footsteps and called out.

"Wait there," he said. He gathered up the bullets in a cloth and walked to the opposite exit if the barn. He walked around and saw Veronique, dressed and ready.

"Goddamn, darlin'," he said smiling. "I love when you're in a dress, but you look damn fine in my clothes too."

She smiled.

"I fear I shall never say the same of you, lover."

He laughed.

"Too big for your dresses anyway," he said, giving her a kiss. "You ready to load up?"

She nodded. They walked back to the porch and loaded the guns with the bullets.

Veronique took her pistol and aimed it at the weathervane on top of the barn. She fired. The cock's head flew off.

"Well they fire," Wall said. "That's good. But stop shootin'"

"The gun?" she asked.

"The weathervane," he said. "They ain't easy to come by,"

"Make a new one," she said.

"I don't want to make a new one, I liked that one."

"I'm scared, Tom." Veronique said.

He put a hand on her shoulder.

"Me too."

A shot rang out from the roof followed by another one.

The two shots took out more of the weathervane.

Tom frowned as Veronique smiled.

"Hey," he called to the roof. "You wanna stop shooting Daddy's goddamn weathervane please?"

Giggles came from the room.

"Just like your Momma," he said. "See anything yet darlin'?"

"Nope," came the response. "I'll let you know."

Veronique reloaded her gun.

"She really is a good shot," she said.

"You both are," he said. "And I really hope this works."

"We'll win," she said, looking at him.

"Always do, don't we?"

She smiled.

"So far,"

"Alright then," he said, finished loading his pistol. "Get inside and wait. And don't go in the barn."

"Yes sir," she said, kissing him. He kissed her back, deeply.

"I love you," she said.

"Love you back." He replied.

He walked from the porch and got on his horse. He rode off, hoping to intercept Trask and at least be able to lure him back to the barn.

That was his hope.

***

Melissa Givens had been called "pleasantly plump" by most of the patrons of the store and she had always been fine with that. It was true. She was rather pleasant almost to a fault. However, this strange man in her store had flat out called her fat.

Fat.

This stung and it took most of the pleasantness right out of her. He lumbered around the store as if he owned the place.

"Well," he said. "You're quite the fat one."

He didn't say it in a mean way; it was said so matter of fact, that it nearly sounded like a compliment. She hemmed and hawed as he strolled back and forth through the store. Finally, she could no longer stand it and said in a loud voice.

"What are you looking for?"

The man turned and smiled.

"I've waited damn near a full minute to see if you'd ask me what I was looking for," he said. "What kind of service do you call that?"

"You called me fat," she said, folding her arms.

He laughed.

"Well, you *are*." He said, walking back towards her. "Isn't a bad thing, ma'am. Just an observation."

"Well, it's damn rude." She said.

"Oh well, I apologize." He said coming up to the counter. "I certainly didn't mean to offend you. I'm not accustomed to seeing a woman of your...stature is all."

"What's that supposed to mean?"

"It means I don't see a lot of fat people." He said, dropping the smile. "I see people more in control of themselves. Then I see someone like you, just prancing around like you're important when all you are is fat."

Her face went red. She wasn't just hurt, she was angry.

"You get on out of my store, you here?" she said.

"No, I need some information from you."

"I said get out!"

The man reached over with both hands and grabbed Melissa by the neck. He lifted her up and over the counter. This didn't happen without maximum discomfort for Melissa. She couldn't breathe and her sheer weight pulled down, hurting her neck. He set her on her feet and she buckled.

"You're going to tell me where I can find the Walls."

She grabbed her neck and coughed.

"You bastard," she said in a grizzled voice. "Oh, you bastard,"

"Tom Wall. His wife. Their whelp. Where?"

"You can go plum to hell," she said and turned away from him, attempting to run. He grabbed a handful of skin on the back of her neck and held her there. She tried to scream, but again, her air supply had been cut.

"My name is Stephan Trask," he said. "You know who I am. You're going to tell me where they are, or I'm going to kill everyone in this goddamn town. Starting with your fat self."

Melissa's face went redder and her eyes began to bulge.

CHAPTER 12

Wall was only about a mile away when he saw a lone rider watching him. He couldn't see features, but the way he sat in the saddle, he knew almost instantly who it was.

Henry Robb.

He figured it had been about three years since he last saw Henry and he was encouraged to see him now. He kicked his horse to ride out and meet him. Looked like Robb had the same idea. When the gap had been closed enough, Wall stopped.

Robb didn't.

Wall sat there wondering what the hell he was trying to do and by the time he figured it out, Robb's horse slammed into his and Wall went flying to the ground.

It knocked the wind out of him, but before he knew it, Robb was on him, picked him up by his collar and threw him about twenty feet.

Wall curled up so he didn't land flat. He tucked and rolled a little and sprang to his feet. He stood up quickly and glared at Robb.

"What in the goddamn hell is this about, Henry?" Wall yelled.

"I'm sorry, Captain." Robb said.

"Sorry about what?"

"About what I have to do,"

Wall shook his head. The wind was still knocked out of him a bit and he needed to get the world to stop spinning.

"Yeah? What the hell is that? You find Trask?"

"Trask sent me to kill you," Robb said. "I figured you might be looking to head him off."

"Damn right," Wall said. "But that don't explain what the hell this is. Where's Bob?"

"Bob's dead," Robb said, putting his head down. He coughed a little bit. "I...I ate him."

"What?"

"Trask...*turned* me into whatever the hell he is," Robb said. "Made me eat Bob."

This took a lot of the anger at Robb away from Wall. He slumped, but kept his hand on his gun.

"I'm sorry, Henry." Wall said. "But you ain't got to do what he wants you to do, you know that, right?"

Robb didn't look up.

"He said he'd kill me," Robb said.

"You can fight him,"

"No," Robb said. "I can't. I don't want to live like this, Tom. I surely don't, but I ain't got no choice."

"There's always a choice," Wall said.

Robb looked up and glared at Wall.

"Sometimes there really ain't," he said. "I reckon if I kill you maybe he'll kill me. I don't think I could be like this forever."

"Well, I got bad news for you. You ain't killing me today, Henry."

Robb nodded.

"I don't see how you're gonna get past me," Robb said.

Wall's eyes narrowed into a cruel expression.

"I ain't fixin' to go past you," he said. "I'll go right through you if I have to."

"You ain't never faced nothing like me before, Tom."

"I've met more folks like you than you have. Now, where the hell is Trask?"

"He's already here," Robb said.

Wall drew his gun.

Robb laughed.

"If that's true, you know that won't do much."

"Maybe, but I'm pretty goddamn clever," Wall said and fired. The bullet hit Robb in the shoulder. Robb stepped back, but his expression didn't change.

"That ain't gonna kill me," Robb said and tried to smile. However, a moment later, the wound began to smoke and Robb began to shake.

"What the hell," Robb said as he began to smoke from his skin. "What did you *do?*"

Wall shot Robb three more times, this time directly in the chest. After a delay, those wounds began to smoke too. Robb began to scream.

Wall ran over to Robb just as Robb collapsed onto the ground, writhing.

"Told you I was clever," Wall said, holstering his gun.

Robb was smoking from every exposed piece of skin. His face began to shrivel and blacken.

"Captain," Robb began. "I'm sorry. I hope you don't hold it against me,"

"I'm sorry too, Henry." Wall said as the man began to crackle and smoke even more. "It weren't your fault."

Robb was smoking as if he were on fire. It looked like he wanted to scream but couldn't quite make the sound. He looked up at Wall and opened his mouth.

"Kill that son of a bitch, Captain,"

Robb began to scream in agony until Wall aimed at Robb's head and pulled the trigger. The smoking continued, but at least Robb wasn't screaming anymore.

Robb was a damn good Ranger, Wall thought. Now he had one more reason to kill this bastard Trask.

And thanks to Robb, he knew his plan would work.

He watched Robb turn to dust and then grabbed his horse. It was more than likely that Trask had gotten to the ranch. He would have to haul ass to get there and took off.

***

Trask finished eating Melissa. He was surprised no one had come into the store. He had held her up and peeled her skin as she screamed in agony. Of course she had told him where Viorica lived. She told him right away, even before he started peeling her skin. But he did it anyway. He was going to have to learn to control these things, but there was too much to do, too much for him to feel with the coming reckoning with Viorica.

He'd sent Robb to kill Wall, which was good of him. It was a good test, to see if Robb would do as he asked. If he did, then he would know that he'd truly been right about him.

He also didn't want to see Wall.

He was beneath him, after all. Viorica's plaything didn't deserve death at the hands of God.

He ate Melissa and ate well. Fat, to be sure, but delicious as well. Maybe, if this town had more fat people, he could save them for food. The town of the new order would feast well right off the bat. Who couldn't love a God who provided that?

No one, that's who.

He smiled and looked around the store. It looked nice. Perhaps he and Robb would come back and see what they wanted, but the day was getting long. He needed to end this. He was at full strength and he was primed and ready to go.

CHAPTER 13

Trask stepped out of the store and ran until he got about a hundred or so feet from the Wall's barn. From there, he could see the house, another two hundred feet from where he stood. Very simple, very plain.

He hated it.

He smiled and spread his arms out.

"*Viorica!*" he called. "I'm here for you!"

The last of his voice's echo rang out loudly and was met with a gun shot. He laughed until the bullet hit him in the knee. After a moment, it began to burn.

His eyes went wide with shock as he looked to see where the shot had come from. He heard a gun reloading and his eyes darted to the roof of the house. He saw the girl. She had a rifle and was aiming it again. He heard her pull the trigger, but nothing happened.

"You must be the *whelp*," Trask called out through his teeth. He couldn't understand why his knee hurt so badly. Gunshots didn't feel like this.

"Go away," the girl cried out. "Or I'll shoot you again."

Trask moved quickly to the back of the barn.

"I'm here for your mother," he called out.

"She don't want to see you," she yelled back. "So go away before my Daddy gets back."

"I'm afraid your Daddy's dead, little girl."

***

Josephine heard this and tried not to cry. She knew it wasn't true and Momma had told her he would say anything to shake her up.

"Nothing kills my Daddy," she said. "So you just turn around get out of here."

She pulled the trigger, but the bullet was somehow stuck. This too, was what her Daddy had feared.

Trask walked back into view.

"I think you'll find," Trask said. "That your gun is a little jammed up."

"I think you'll find mine *isn't*," Veronique said, firing her gun directly at Trask's head from about five feet from behind him. He dodged, but barely. The bullet scraped his temple but Trask had vanished.

Veronique narrowed her eyes and followed.

Trask had run behind the house.

"Come on now, Viorica," he said. "You don't really think you can kill me do you?"

"It's *Veronique*," Josephine said from the roof. Her slingshot was poised and she fired. It was so unexpected, the rock caught him in his shoulder. It had driven itself about halfway into his shoulder and he screamed. He ran out of shock.

"Dang," Josephine said, getting another rock.

He ran back to the barn.

"Viorica, please stop this. I came to talk." He said.

"No you didn't," she yelled from the opposite side of the barn. "You don't kill that many people to just *talk*."

"Fair enough," Trask said. "But you know you can't hope to win. You've done impressively so far, but you're finished. So is your daughter."

There were two loud pops from the barn as Josephine fired two more rocks in quick succession. From inside the barn she heard Trask roar in agony.

"Got him again!" Josephine squealed from the roof.

Trask was furious. He'd never been hit like this by anything in hundreds of years.

"You're all going to die!" he screamed.

***

"Not today," Veronique said, rounding the corner and shooting. This time, he managed to dodge all of them and rounded the whole barn until he was behind her. He punched her as hard as he could in the back of her head. This sent her flying. She managed to recover, but by the time she put her arms down to stand, he was on her. He punched her twice in the head as Josephine screamed from the roof. She grabbed another stone and set it up, but as she aimed, he vanished.

Suddenly, she felt a sharp pain in her head and she flew off of the roof. She fell and landed right in front of the porch steps. She cried out in pain.

Standing on the roof, Trask began to change.

His whole body shook and transformed quickly. Veronique rolled over and sat up to watch this.

He had gotten bigger. He must've just eaten, she thought. She looked at Josephine. The fall wouldn't hurt her too badly, but she was scared now and crying. She saw a gash on Josephine's arm. It was probably broken.

Angry, Veronique began to change as well as quickly as she could. She hoped she could do this as quickly as Trask.

***

Josephine's cried stopped as she watched her mother transform. She struggled to sit up to watch but she couldn't. Her arm and everything hurt very badly.

"Go under the porch," said Pajkov from behind her. "Quickly!" Josephine did her best to crawl under the porch. It was slower than she wanted, but she managed.

Once there, she crawled over to where she knew the daffodils were.

"Hello?" she cried. "Pajkov?"

"I'm here," the spider said. "So are the others. You'll need to be quiet."

"But Momma…"

"She can handle herself," Pajkov said. "You hush now."

***

Trask had finished changing and jumped off of the roof. He landed with a very loud thud. He was enormous Fifteen feet high and completely black. He was terrifying to look at and for Veronique that was saying a lot. She was nearly done changing, but she was only ten feet high and not nearly as bulky. Formidable to be sure, but not nearly as powerful as Trask.

Trask attacked first, biting Veronique's neck and tossing her thirty feet into the side of the barn. She broke some of the boards and a few of her ribs. The spider like exoskeleton only protected so much. She got back up and was picked up again. This time, she was slammed hard on the ground.

"This is it, Viorica." Trask snarled. "You don't get away anymore. You'll regret leaving me."

"I will *never* regret leaving you," she said. She saw the leg that Josephine had shot. It was still smoking and wounded. She spun and kicked the wound as hard as she could. Trask roared and collapsed. She pulled her mouth to the bottom of the leg and took it in her teeth. She ripped if from his body and he shrieked in agony.

She flung it aside quickly. Veronique scrambled up and ran toward the barn. She got about five feet in front of the door and turned.

"Well come on, then!" she yelled.

"You do not command *God*!" Trask yelled, struggling to his taloned legs.

"You are *not God*!" she yelled and snarled, showing her fangs.

Trask ran full on at Veronique. She tried to time it so she would dodge him, sending him into the barn, but at the last moment, he swerved and grabbed her by the neck. Still running, he leapt into the air with her, then drove her into the ground, his taloned appendages driving into her. She screamed in agony.

***

Wall heard the screams and roars and knew what was happening. He urged the horse on further, but the horse seemed to know what was waiting for him. He kicked the horse again, this time it sped up.

He saw the barn and the side that had been crushed. He knew whatever was happening, was happening in between the house and the barn. He dismounted the horse and ran for the barn, going in the back way.

He closed the door and heard Veronique scream after a large crash. He carefully climbed the structure near the door and looked out through the large hole in the side.

He saw the Trask thing with three taloned appendages stabbing his wife. He pulled his gun and aimed it. He fired three times. The shots knocked Trask over in agony. Veronique tried to crawl away but couldn't she was bleeding freely from the four wounds.

"Trask!" Wall yelled from inside the barn.

Trask who was still writhing in agony, snapped to attention.

"Who is that?" Trask roared.

"Tom Wall, Texas Ranger." Wall said, almost out of habit. "I'm afraid you're not welcome here you murderin' son of a bitch."

Trask managed to finally get on his legs and crawled toward the barn.

"I see you made it against Mr. Robb," Trask said. "You won't have that kind of luck with me."

"I don't need luck," Wall said from inside the barn. "I just reckon there just ain't been nobody who wanted you *goddamn dead enough*. And believe me, I want you dead."

Trask laughed.

"What little trap do you have waiting for me in there, Mr. Wall?"

"Why don't you come in and find out." Wall said. He could kick himself. He figured out the trap although in retrospect, it wasn't really that subtle. He jumped down from where he had climbed. He looked and grabbed one of the jars of jelly on the work table. He also grabbed something long and sharp and tucked it in his pants.

"I'm afraid I'll be too busy, killing your wife, Wall."

Trask changed direction and went to Veronique's body that was now reverting back to its human shape.

Tom ran out of the back barn door. He rounded the corner running, expecting to see Trask going after his wife.

But Trask was gone.

Wall stopped and turned around.

A taloned arm ran him though the gut, lifting him in the air. He dropped his gun and screamed in pain. Trask brought him up to the level of his grotesque face.

"*Charmed* to meet you, Mr. Wall." Trask said.

He looked into Wall's face for fear but was surprised that he saw a man with cold, cruel eyes looking right back at him. He was yelling, but he wasn't afraid.

"Can't say the same," Wall managed. "You like jelly?"

Wall slammed the jar onto the side of Trask's grotesque head. Trask regarded him still smiling until the smeared jelly began to smoke and sizzle. Trask bellowed.

Tom reached into his pocket and pulled out the sharpened branch he'd been carving from the tree. With great effort, he stabbed it into the side of Track's smoldering face. Trask screamed louder and threw him in the direction where Veronique lie squirming. He landed with a thud, grabbing his midsection, hoping his guts could stay where they were for the time being. He crawled over to Veronique's, now mostly back to human form.

Trask had begun to spin in pure agony. He reached up and yanked the branch out of his face. His scream became words as he stood to his full height.

"How *dare* you? How dare you do this to your God!" he said.

***

Josephine crawled out from under the porch, crying but determined. She saw her parents, bloodied but alive and Trask getting closer to them both.

Her arm hurt and hung at a very odd angle, but she managed to stand up. She walked over to the side of the porch.

"Hey," she yelled. The Trask thing turned. "Did you forget about me?"

Trask stopped and looked the little girl.

"Well, look at this," he said, trying to compose himself. "A snack. Should I save you for later?"

She reached into her pocket and pulled out a bullet. Little billows of smoke came from her fingers and she hissed in pain.

Trask laughed.

Josephine smiled a little.

"Ain't no goddamn later for *you*," she said, and brought up her broken arm still holding the slingshot. She quickly loaded it and fired it directly in Trask's grotesque face. She cried out as the force bent her arm in an even more painful direction. She collapsed on the ground, crying.

Trask howled and screamed anew. The hole in his face was gushing blood and smoke. He began to turn around and around again, howling in pain. From behind Josephine, she heard buzzing.

She turned and saw the spiders from the daffodils. Not six, but *thousands* of them. They all marched toward Trask who was still screaming.

The spiders all began to crawl on him, spinning webs and biting. He began to howl less as he realized what was going on.

"What are you *doing*? Get off of me!" he cried. "Stop biting me!"

He began to turn again. Josephine was confused. What was a spider bite going to do?

"You were very smart about the berries," Pajkov said. Josephine sat up and looked down. The yellow orb spider sat next to her.

"Thanks, but I don't think the spiders bites are gonna help." She said, holding her arm and crying.

"Well, that's where you're wrong." The spider said. "We eat the bug that lives in that tree. They eat the berries all year around. So, whatever they get of the berry is inside of us."

Josephine understood and she smiled.

Trask felt the burning pour through him a bite at a time. He screamed and flailed at the spiders to no avail. He was getting light headed and dizzy.

This couldn't be what was killing him.

He *couldn't* die.

He was God.

He was...

Who *was* he?

His entire body felt like it was on fire and burning.

The pain was unbearable.

He roared one last time as his entire body began to dissolve and turn to dust. His last thought was that if he was God, where was he going?

Josephine watched all of the spiders gently touch down onto the ground and scamper towards the porch. She heard them talking about what had just happened.

"Thank you!" Josephine squealed happily. "Thank you!"

Pajkov crawled up her arm and onto her face.

"Goodbye, little one." She said to the little girl. "I'll never forget you or your family."

"Why do you have to go?"

"There are a lot of spiders here," the spider said, crawling down her arm. "I need to move on if I'm going to eat."

Josephine chuckled.

"Will my Daddy and Momma be okay?" She looked at her parents who were both still staring at the burning wreck of Trask.

"I don't know that child," she said. "You'll need to check on them."

"Will I ever talk to you again?"

"Perhaps, one day..." he said. "If you need us."

Pajkov crawled past the daffodils and into the elsewhere.

Josephine got up carefully to check on her parents.

EPILOGUE

Corpus Christi, Texas 1896

Josephine was standing in front of the barn with her slingshot. She took a rock, loaded it and carefully aimed it almost straight into the air. She pulled it back and let it go. The rock made a whistling sound as it rose up. The sound stopped and then began to whistle again as it came back down.

The rock came back down on top of the mangled weathervane and drove it straight through the top of the barn. It landed on the floor of the barn with a crash. Josephine gave a loud yell and laughed.

The baby boy in the little stroller laughed as well.

"Look at that, Val!" she said, looking down at the baby boy. "I did it!"

"Josephine, what did I tell you about Daddy's weathervane?" Veronique yelled from inside the house.

Josephine stopped laughing and looked at the doorway.

"It's alright, darlin'" Wall said from the porch. "She's praticin' her aim."

Veronique came to the door and walked out, limping a little bit.

"Aren't you the one who said that was a gift and how much you liked that thing?" she said, smirking.

"I reckon, we could just get a new one," Wall said. He got up from his chair slowly. The wounds from last year still hurt, and the doc said he'd never be at a hundred percent, but he was alive and that was good enough.

He walked to his wife and grabbed her.

"Come here woman, give me a kiss." He said smiling.

"When you say things like that," she said smiling back. "It makes me think you want a lot more kids than we currently have."

"Well, by God darlin'," he said looking into her eyes. "What in the world would be wrong with that?"

He kissed her deeply and she kissed him back.

She pulled away from him, smiling.

"I wonder what comes next for us, Tom." She said, a small look of concern crossing her face. "We've survived so much. What's next?"

Tom looked at her, then at the two children.

"More of this I reckon." He said. "And I'm alright with that."

"As am I," she said. She smiled.

They both heard another rock hit the weathervane when Josephine called out.

"Mail!" she said excitedly.

Tom and Veronique looked and saw that Mark Tanner, the pony express rider was riding over to the house. He waved and smiled broadly.

"Howdy, folks," he called.

"Mark, good to see you." Tom said. "Anything good today?"

"Well," Mark said, galloping over to the porch. Tom walked over to him and stuck out his hand. They shook firmly. "I'm guessing about this. It might be for your missus, but it's an odd name."

"What's so odd about it?"

"Well, it ain't her's. See for yourself," Mark said, handing the letter to Veronique. She looked at it and her face went pale. She dropped the letter.

Tom frowned. He bent down with some effort and picked up the letter.

He looked at the envelope.

It was from Romania.

It was addressed to Viorica Muresan.

The End

ACKNOWLEDGEMENTS

Much love and thanks to the three ladies who always put up with me somehow; Deb, Annabelle and Samantha Pyles. I love youse...

The cover and artwork for this book was created by Jeanette Andromeda. She is also responsible for suggesting that a full length novel about these characters would be a good thing. The art is beautiful and terrifying. Everything you want to see on a book cover. Check out her work at jeanettecreations.com. Thank you, Jeanette.

Huge thanks to Emma Ennis, one of my favorite writers who helped in the edit of this book. You are fecking awesome!

A very big thanks to Daniel Knauf for showing the way to put this book together so long ago. Thanks for the invaluable insight, my friend.

Special shout out to the Texas Ranger Hall of Fame and Museum for their really cool and informative website which helped a lot in some of the things about such a legendary group. Check them out at http://www.texasranger.org/.

Special thanks to Rona Walter, Jesse J. Saxon, Justi Hillberry, Rochelle Delgado, Meagan Fisher, Daniel Foytik, and C. Bryan Brown.

Thanks to Jon Towers, Melanie Friedrich, Tony "Prog Squatch" Rowsick, and all at Society 13.

Much love and affection to the work of Larry McMurtry, Cormac McCarthy, Joe R. Lansdale, Neil Gaiman, Stephen King and especially Mark Twain.

A very big thank you to Gary Lee Vincent for again, taking a shot on my work. You rock, sir.

And of course, to you dear reader. As always, thank *you*.

忠

ABOUT THE AUTHOR

Nelson W Pyles is an author living in Pittsburgh PA. He has written two novels, published several short stories and has written several episodes of the popular audio drama *The Lift*. He is also the creator of The Wicked Library Podcast, a musician and a narrator.

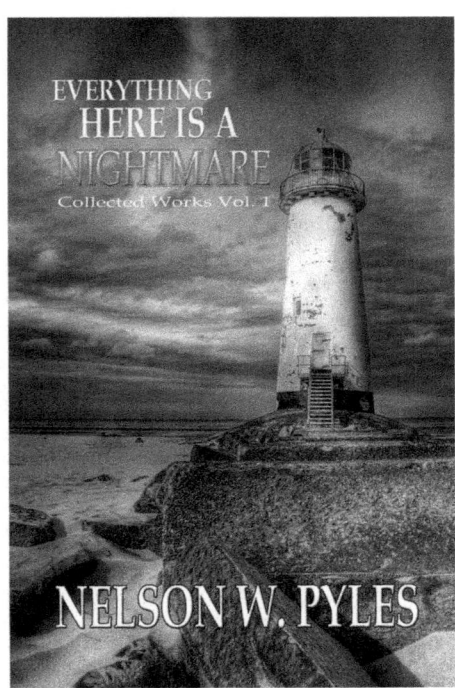

EVERYTHING HERE IS A NIGHTMARE
Collected Works Vol 1.

"Pyles makes it look easy. His characters come instantly alive with the cocksure verve and swagger of rock stars."
  - Daniel Knauf, creator of HBO's "Carnivale,"
  Executive Producer/Writer, ABC's "The Blacklist."

The critically acclaimed author of Demons, Dolls and Milkshakes returns with fifteen tales of horror and suspense with Everything Here is a Nightmare.

From zombies in the old west, to a young boy tempted by the Devil. From vampires with romantic longing, to an abandoned lighthouse haunted by vengeful spirits. From a serial killer getting unholy justice, to a haunted English race car, Nelson W Pyles invites you to explore a landscape of fear, suspense and horror.

Take his hand and hold on tight. Remember that whatever you find here, whatever you see, no matter what you might think it could be... know this: Everything Here is a Nightmare.

Burning Bulb
PUBLISHING

ANTHOLOGIES
BIZARRO AND TRANSGRESSIVE FICTION

THE BIG BOOK OF BIZARRO

The Big Book of Bizarro brings together the peculiar prose of an international cast of the most grotesquely-gonzo, genre-grinding modern writers who ever put pen to paper (or mouse to pad), including:

NIGHT OF THE LIVING DEAD horror writers John Russo & George Kosana; HUSTLER MAGAZINE erotica contributors Eva Hore, Andrée Lachapelle, & J. Troy Seate and established Bizarro genre authors D. Harlan Wilson, William Pauley III, Wol-vriey, Laird Long, Richard Godwin and so many more!

From Alien abductions to Zombie sex, The Big Book of Bizarro contains OVER FIFTY STORIES of the most outrélandish transgressive fiction that you'll ever lay your capricious and curious hands upon!

WESTWARD HOES

Nine outlaw writers rode into town from obscurity to pen nine tantalizing tales of horror and fantasy, and leaving once they branded their own personal marks on the weird western genre and became living legends of the American Frontier experience.

Like drunken Indian scouts, the writers fervidly tracked down and captured the Western genre, tore off its fashionable veneer and ravished its exposed essence.

So belly up to the bar with your favorite soiled dove and enjoy perusing these thrilling tales of Old West debauchery, danger and desire; compiled by the publisher of The Big Book of Bizarro and featuring the bizarro novella *Big Trouble in Little Ass* by Wol-vriey.

Burning Bulb
PUBLISHING

GARY LEE VINCENT'S
DARKENED
THE WEST VIRGINIA VAMPIRE SERIES

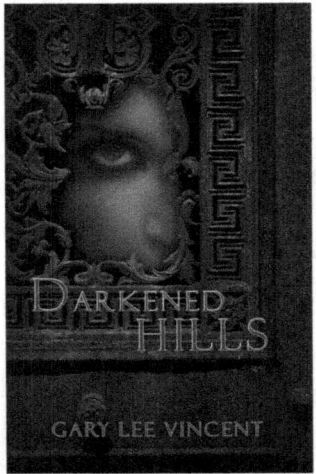

DARKENED HILLS

When evil descends on a small West Virginia town, who will survive?

Jonathan did not start out his life to become a rambler, it justworked out that way. William was a troubled youth with something to hide. Both were from Melas, a small town tucked away in the West Virginia hills... a town where disappearances are happening more and more frequently.

After the suicide of a wanted serial killer, the townsfolk thought the nightmare was over. But when a centuries-old vampire is discovered they find out the hard way it's just getting started. Dark secrets can only stay hidden for so long and when the devil comes to collect, there will be hell to pay. Can Jonathan and William find a way to stop the vampire before it's too late? Find out in *Darkened Hills!*

DARKENED HOLLOWS

In the heart-stopping sequel to the award-winning *Darkened Hills*, Jonathan and William must return to West Virginia to face possible criminal charges stemming from their last visit to the damned town of Melas, where both had narrowly escaped the clutches of a vampire seethe.

And as livestock start mysteriously getting murdered with all of their blood drained, worried farmers are searching for answers - leaving the local Sheriff and his deputy racing against time to learn the cause before a more violent crime is committed.

Burning Bulb
PUBLISHING

WWW.DARKENEDHILLS.COM

GARY LEE VINCENT'S
DARKENED
THE WEST VIRGINIA VAMPIRE SERIES

DARKENED WATERS

When the world goes to hell, the chosen must arise!

As Talman Cane orchestrates a flood of epic proportions in this third installment of the *Darkened* series the towns of Melas and Tarklin are caught completely off guard by the deluge. Hell-bent on finishing what they started, the evil brothers return to the lunatic asylum to take care of the witnesses and add to the ever-growing army of the undead.

Aided by Lucifer himself and the insane vampire demon Legion, the stage is set to channel all of the forces of hell to come forth. In an all-out race to survive, Jonathan, William, and Amanda soon discover they are up against impossible odds as Lucifer opens the Gateway to Hell, ushering in the zombie apocalypse and the End Times.

Find out who will survive this cosmic battle of the ages in *Darkened Waters!*

DARKENED SOULS

Melas and the Madison House are about to be rebuilt.
True evil is about to be reborne!

Young ex-priest and vampire-killer William is drawn back to the West Virginian town that almost killed him, where his vampire arch-enemy Victor Rothenstein still stalks the earth.

The town of Melas lies destroyed after the battle of the End of Days. But why is wealthy Jackie Nixon so eager to rebuild it using the bone dust of murdered souls?

Terrible evil has visited before, but the Gateway to Hell is about to be reopened in a horrific climax. And this time – it's personal.

www.DARKENEDHILLS.com

Burning Bulb
PUBLISHING

GARY LEE VINCENT'S
DARKENED
THE WEST VIRGINIA VAMPIRE SERIES

DARKENED MINDS

Jackie Nixon intends to become Vampire Queen, but at what blood-drenched cost?

In this continuation to the explosive infernal saga begun in Darkened Souls, newly-turned vampire Jackie Nixon is taking no prisoners. Accompanied by her daughter, Kate, and by the captive vampire lord Victor Rothenstein, Jackie Nixon explores the Darkness. There, she intends to rouse the slumbering vampire race, bound under an ancient curse, and with their help, rule the human world.

But there's a deadly threat to Jackie's plans. Not just William who is trying to stop her, but her own royal ambitions. If Jackie performs the ritual to wake the sleeping vampires the wrong way, she could instead free the Red Beast of Hell, an unspeakable evil that even the undead fear.

DARKENED DESTINIES

With over 45 people missing after Jackie Nixon's party, the mysteries surrounding Melas and the Madison House keep getting darker.

Now, with legions of vampires at her command, can anything or anyone stop her from gaining complete control over all mankind?

The final battle has begun! As the Vampire Queen ascends her throne and sets to unleash the full forces of darkness, the fate of all things good hangs in the balance.

Burning Bulb
PUBLISHING

WWW.DARKENEDHILLS.COM

DAVID J. FAIRHEAD

"David Fairhead writes compelling stories that offer very human characters and very inhuman monsters. There is no subtlety in Fairhead's imagination - he is simply dying to scare the hell out of you." - Nelson W Pyles author of DEMONS, DOLLS AND MILKSHAKES

THE FALL

Hopelessness... How do you protect your loved ones when Hell itself opens its insidious mouth?

Horror... Nightmarish Creatures invade your world and there is nowhere to hide.

Blood... How long can you hold out before they come for you?

Pain... Where do you run to avoid being eaten alive by monsters with a voracious appetite for your flesh?

Screams... While you selfishly run for your own life.

Questions... Who is to blame? Where did they come from? How many people survived...and how does the human race find the means to fight back?

THE FALL OF TOMORROW is man's last tale of desperation told by those that are striving to salvage some hope against a ravenous bastion of evil beasts bent on ruling our world.

DWELLING IN THE DARK

From David J. Fairhead, author of the FALL OF TOMORROW, comes DWELLING IN THE DARK- A soulful anthology of creeping terror to keep you up in the small hours with horror set in the past, present and future. Overlapping bits of puzzle fitting each other, before and after The Fall of Tomorrow.

A place where three children facing a monstrous foe can only pray that their bloody summer would just come to an end. Go back to the 1960's- THE COMMUNE where overindulging hippies use a mage's diary to control the end of the world, only to see first-hand that their drug induced visions have horrific ramifications. Where a young boy's visit to a haunted house becomes a lesson in RESIDUAL morality. The story, DEEPER- plunges two brothers into a sinkhole only to find they were being hunted by an insidious creature from its depths. Visit the old west as hero Dekker Collins battles evil gunslingers in DEMONEYE.

And so much more...!

Burning Bulb
PUBLISHING

WWW.*FAIRLYDARKPRODUCTIONS*.COM

WEST VIRGINIA-THEMED HUMORROROTICA

BY RICH BOTTLES JR.

HELLHOLE WEST VIRGINIA

From the heights of Mothman's perch high atop the Silver Bridge in Point Pleasant to the depths of Hellhole Cavern in Pendleton County, evil lurks within the shadows as the sun sets upon the haunted hills and hollows of West Virginia.

Bizarro author Rich Bottles Jr. blows the coffin lid off horror genre clichés with this tour de force cast of Eco-friendly vampires, beach-yearning zombies and sex-starved she-devils.

LUMBERJACKED

If you are easily offended or do not possess a truly depraved sense of humor, this story may not be the light summer reading fare you desire. As for the four feisty female freshmen stranded on top of West Virginia's third highest mountain, they have no choice but to experience the sick, twisted debauchery and perverted mayhem described deep inside the tight unbroken bindings of this horrific missive.

Lumberjacked takes the reader to a nightmarish world where character development and aesthetic integrity are prematurely cut short by the swinging axes of maniacal lumberjacks, who are hell bent on death and destruction in the remote forests of Appalachia. And at the climax, when paranoia crosses over to the paranormal, Lumberjacked makes Deliverance look like a family raft trip down the Lower Gauley.

THE MANACLED

What happens when twin brothers lease out the former West Virginia State Penitentiary with the false purpose of filming a documentary on supernatural phenomena, but their true intention is to make a pornographic movie?

Chaos ensues as the disturbed spirits of murdered convicts, along with the reanimated dead from the neighboring Indian Burial Mound, take their vengeance on the unwary and undressed trespassers.

Zombies, ghosts, mobsters and porn collide in this bizarro tale from horror author Rich Bottles Jr.

Burning Bulb
PUBLISHING

WEST VIRGINIA-THEMED HUMORROROTICA

BY RICH BOTTLES JR.

BY

A collection of short stories from Rich Bottles Jr. Be forewarned that the graphic sex and violence described in this book of bizarre short stories may provoke psychological or emotional triggers for some unstable or weak-minded readers, including, but not limited to, the following extreme content: Rape, Torture, Murder, Mayhem, Kidnapping, Cannibalism, Necrophilia, Poisoning, Prostitution, Pornography, Nazis, War Crimes, Ethnic Cleansing, Terrorism, Incarceration, Bondage & Discipline, Sadomasochism, Corporal Punishment, Foot Fetishism, Masturbation, Alcoholism, Drug Abuse, Eating Disorders, Domestic Violence, Mental Illness, Suicide, Drowning, Religious Intolerance, The Occult, Adult Language, Homosexuality, Sodomy, Unwanted Pregnancy, Amputees, Adultery, Incest, Shoplifting, Bukkake, Penis Envy, Cigarette Smoking, and Heavy Metal Music.

THE VAMPIRE WHO SAVES CHRISTMAS

Cantankerous demon Krampus is out to ruin Christmas for everyone, but Mrs. Claus and Jolly Ole Saint Nicholas will do everything in their power to stop his diabolical plan, even if it means becoming vampires to fight the evil villain! Join Alfie the Elf, Rudolpho the Reindeer Trainer, and all the other merry residents of Christmasland in this hilarious yuletide adventure that is sure to become a joyous holiday classic!

THE TAILSMAN

He's hot on the trail, looking for some tail! Follow the adventures of Sly Franko in this ornery comic book set in the *Westward Hoes* universe by Gary Lee Vincent, Rich Bottles Jr., and Stuart Brown.

Burning Bulb
PUBLISHING

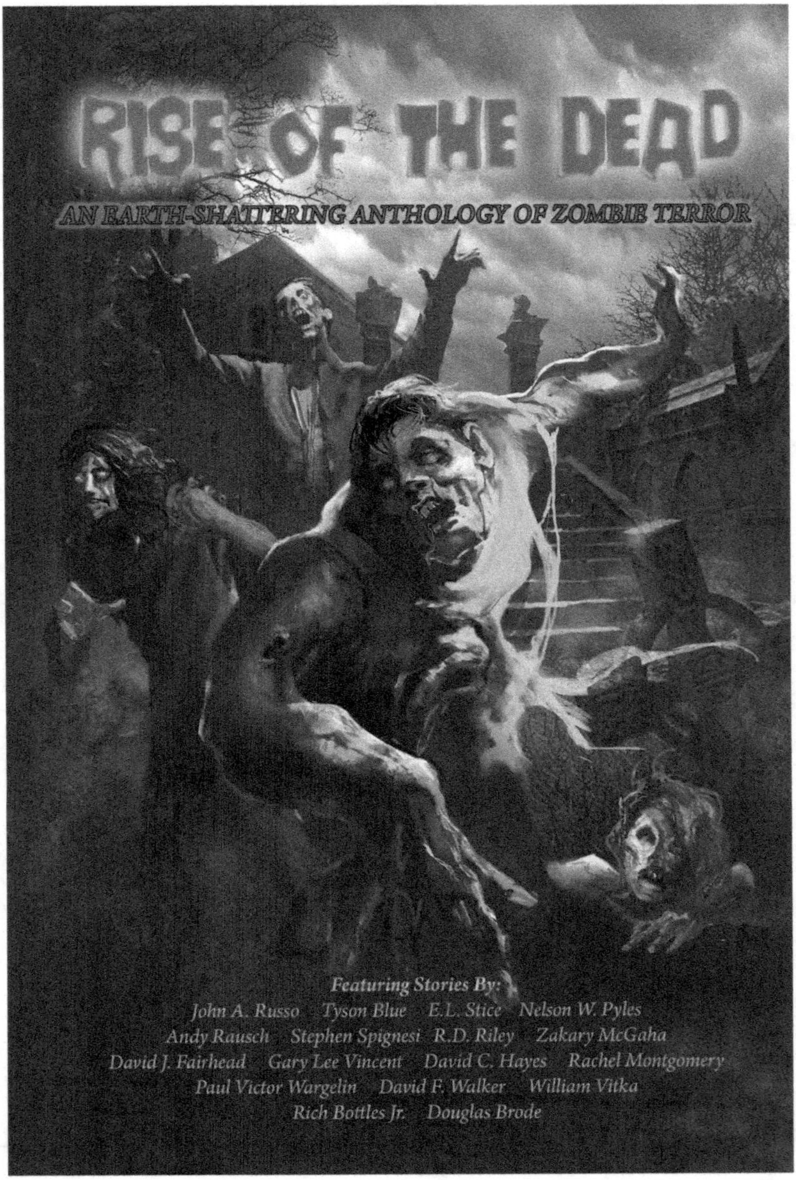

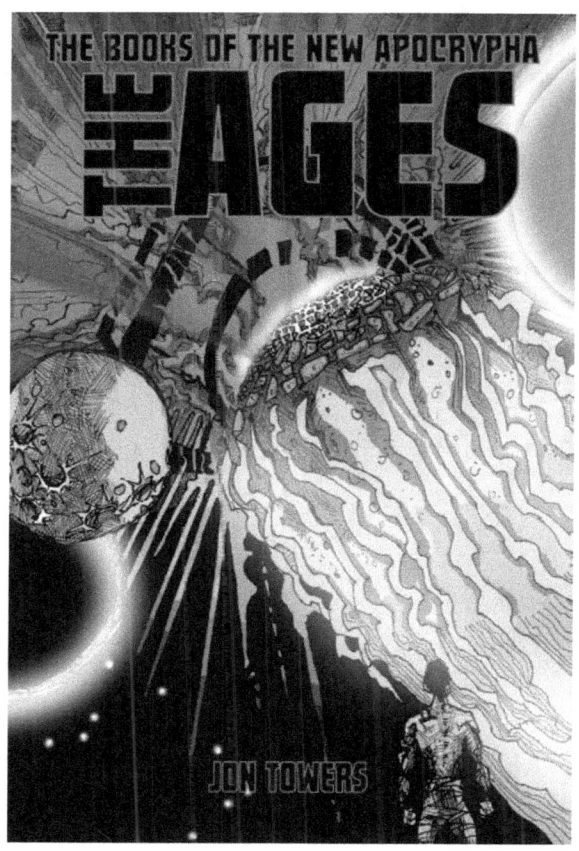

THE BOOKS OF THE NEW APOCRYPHA
THE AGES

JON TOWERS

"A masterful, compelling journey through time, 'The Ages' delves deep into arcane knowledge, myth, and legend. The art is stunning, and the story takes you on a journey where mortals, immortals, angels, and demons are all forced to deal with the folly that is God's creation. It's a beautifully dark and gritty ride through history."
–Daniel Foytik host: The Lift, The Wicked Library

The Ages begins with the shocking story of Cain and Abel, and the journey of violence and revenge spanning thousands of years, following Cain through his cursed life from an ancient invasion of malicious angels, to the American Revolutionary war. This four-part story follows the astrological procession of the ages and shows how each 2,500 year age parallels major changes on the development of Earth's inhabitants. Cain's blasphemous struggle with the divine and sacred tyrant God will create and crumble empires, shape history and cause a cosmic cataclysm.

ANTHOLOGIES
BIZARRO AND TRANSGRESSIVE FICTION

THE BIG BOOK OF BIZARRO SPECIAL KINDLE EDITIONS

OTHER AWESOME COLLECTIONS

 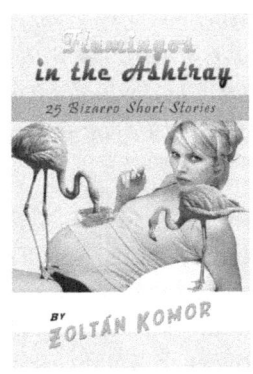 

Burning Bulb
PUBLISHING

WOL-VRIEY
BIZARRO AND TRANSGRESSIVE FICTION

GIRLS ARE NOT SMILING

Welcome To The Road Trip From Hell

Pagan is demon-possessed.

Lori is suicidal.

Britt is just terminally pissed off.

Meet three young Boston women on the run from the law, each with problems that will fuse into more than the sum of their individual parts, becoming a holocaust of sex and violence and terror, a literal rain of blood and horror and gore and evil.

And if that wasn't already bad enough, Pagan's pet demon is slowly transforming her into something both unspeakable and unholy. Truly, these girls aren't smiling.

BLUE NIGHTMARES

Consummate EVIL is coming. It is relentless and unavoidable. It is Blue.

Jessica Schreiber is seeing things. Very horrible things. Since arriving in Raynham for what should have been a relaxing vacation, she's been seeing *The Big Blue*.

Jessica is smelling things too—dead and rotting things that she can't see. She is sure those dead and rotting things are dead people. Lots of dead people.

Jessica's worst nightmares will soon become her reality. Her reality will soon become a terrifying nightmare.

The tentacled residents of the House of Death have a lot that they wish to show Jessica Schreiber. They have a lot that they wish to tell her. But will she survive long enough to learn their lessons?

Burning Bulb
PUBLISHING

David J. Fairhead Presents

FIENDS
OF THE FLESH

David J. Fairhead   Jon Towers   Nelson W. Pyles
Rich Bottles Jr.   M.K. Oster   Solon Tsangaras
Michelle Bowser   Paul Wargelin   James Castiglione   Bill Smith